CH00870549

Reflect:
Snow White
Retold

DEMELZA CARLTON

A tale in the Romance a Medieval Fairy Tale series

This is a work of fiction. Names, characters, businesses, places, events and incidents are either the products of the author's imagination or used in a fictitious manner. Any resemblance to actual persons, living or dead, or actual events is purely coincidental.

Copyright © 2018 Demelza Carlton

Lost Plot Press

All rights reserved.

ISBN-13: 978-1-925799-22-4

ISBN-10: 1-925799-22-0

DEDICATION

For Geraldine, because Snow White always was her
favourite.

One

Guinevere whirled around in panic when her door slammed. The whirr of doves in flight signalled the departure of her friends. She envied them their easy escape.

"He's finally gone mad," Xylander said. He strode across the room to close and bar the shutters, engulfing them both in gloom. "You're not safe here any more."

Guinevere pressed a hand to her chest, trying to still her racing heart. She managed a weak smile. "We're his only children. He wouldn't hurt us." Not even she believed it. Or why would she panic so at the slamming of a door?

Xylander shook his head. "You didn't hear him, Guin. He's been trying to arrange marriages for us both. He said if the king you're supposed to marry won't agree on your dowry, he'll cut off your head and hands and send them to him instead."

"A jest, surely."

"He sent for the Master at Arms, demanding his axe, Guin. That was no jest. You must flee." Xylander pressed something into her hands. Sackcloth, it felt like. "Fill this with everything you wish to take with you. I recommend you wear something sturdy and warm, suitable for rough travel, and fill the sack with your court clothes and what jewels you can carry."

She had precious few of those, seeing as her father didn't allow her in court. She had no jewels to speak of, for those that had belonged to her mother had been claimed by her stepmother. As for rough travel…why, she hadn't left the castle grounds in months. The roughest travel she'd known in years was to get a stone in her slipper on the way to the cathedral as she crossed the square. "Xylander, I can't."

He gripped her shoulders. "We must. I will come with you to protect you, Guin, and see you safely to your new kingdom. You will be a queen, just like Mother was."

Her little brother protecting her. A few years ago, it would have been a funny notion, but Xylander had become a man while she became a mouse.

"What will we eat? Where will we sleep?" she asked. And what would become of the castle in her absence? She'd been chatelaine since her mother's death.

"We will bring as much food as we can carry in our saddlebags, and I can hunt along the way. I will pitch you a hunting camp as comfortable as your tower room here, I promise."

She wanted to believe him. Oh, the comfort was likely a lie, for nothing beat her feather bed atop its straw mattress, though the straw was wearing thin now. They must be due to be refilled – something else she'd planned to do this week. Could she trust the maids to do the work without her?

No, it was her brother she would have to trust, because she'd be leaving the beds and the maids behind.

She did believe Xylander about the hunting part, for the guards had taken to calling him Xylander the Huntsman, and the bards told stories of his victories on feast days. When her father allowed it, of course. More and more often lately, he'd roar at the bard for getting some detail wrong and send the poor man out of the hall for a flogging.

Come to think of it, there hadn't been any bard at the last feast she'd been allowed to attend. Even the travelling minstrels had stayed clear, not willing to risk being flogged to death for some imagined slight.

Xylander was right. Her heart knew it, but her head had just needed a moment to catch up.

"Bring me boys' garb. Something your squire would wear, so that when we ride out of the gates together, no one will think to look twice at me," Guinevere said. She thought a moment, then added, "Don't forget a cloak, for if I must look like a queen when we arrive, I cannot cut my hair, and I will need a cloak to cover it."

Xylander nodded. "I had thought to wait for nightfall, but if you wear a disguise, we can leave sooner. You are as brave as you are wise, sister. Any kingdom would be blessed to have you as their queen." He hurried out.

Guinevere let herself sag against the shuttered window. She would have to be a fool to try and flee from her father, who would send his troops out in search of his lost children.

But she would rather take her chances with bandits on the road, than wait for the axe to fall here. A fool she might be, but she'd be a bigger fool if she stayed.

Two

An owl screeched in the night, warning invaders out of its territory.

Guinevere jumped. "What was that?" Her round eyes reflected the firelight, making her look like an owl herself.

Xylander fought not to laugh. "Just a barn owl. I thought you liked birds."

She pulled her cloak more closely around her and lay down again. "I do. I just…never heard one scream like that. It sounds like that poor woman last week, when Father overturned the soup pot in his fury and scalded the cook." She shivered.

Poor Guinevere. With their older brother, Lubos, riding around the kingdom, doing his best to rule in Father's stead, and Xylander out hunting as often as he could, she alone had borne the brunt of their father's rages, along with her duties as castle chatelaine, for their stepmother hadn't the slightest idea how to run a castle.

"You'll be safe inside the walls of your own castle before Father finds out you're gone, and not even he will be mad enough to go to war to get you back," Xylander said.

She rolled onto her side so she faced him. "Where are we going, Lander?"

"To the court of King Artorius, in Castrum. His fortress city is nigh on impregnable, and his knights are the finest anywhere. Father offered him your hand in marriage, so it will not seem strange for you to arrive." Xylander hesitated, but he had to tell her the rest, so he continued, "Artorius has a daughter, but no sons, so he demanded that Father betroth me to his daughter by way of alliance instead. Father wants the girl to come here, to make me his heir and unite the two kingdoms. Artorius wants me to go there, to marry the girl and become king."

"But Lubos is the eldest, and Father's heir!" Guinevere protested.

"Father has gone mad, like I said." Xylander said, throwing a stick at the fire.

"So you're taking me to Artorius, so you can claim your bride? Then what?" she asked.

Xylander shook his head. "Once you are safely crowned, then I can disappear. I have no desire to be king of anywhere, Guin. You know that. I've always left the kingly things to Lubos, because that's his destiny, not mine. I wish I'd been born a knight, or some nobleman, so that I might spend my days hunting. You must call me Lander, or Sir Lander, and if anyone asks, I am your protector, your father's sworn knight. Not a prince."

"And what about the girl? The princess?" Guinevere pressed.

He would stay as far away from her as possible. Xylander forced himself to shrug. "A marriageable girl, whose dowry comes with a whole kingdom, shouldn't be so difficult to deal with, even if she's a gorgon. Find her a more suitable match than me. I'd suggest Lubos, but he had his heart set on some baron's daughter, last time I looked. You'll be her stepmother, so marriage alliances are well within your power to make. Or perhaps she has her own ideas. If she's anything like you, I'm sure she will."

Even if she was still the loveliest woman in the world, nothing would induce Xylander to marry the girl, because her dowry came with a king's crown he had no desire to wear. Better to believe her a gorgon, and never see her again.

"Worry not about the girl, or anything else," he said. "As your brother and your knight protector, I swear on my life I will see that you are safe before I leave you. You will never have to face Father and his axe."

She sighed. "Then you should sleep, too, for you will need to be well rested if we must ride to the next kingdom." She patted the blanket beside her. "Better than sleeping on the floor of my tower room, just like you said." She smiled at her own joke, making light of her discomfort.

Xylander shook his head. "I cannot. Someone must stand watch, and even if I wanted to, I could not sleep, knowing you are in danger." And whenever he closed his eyes, his imagination showed him her headless, handless corpse. Better to stay awake all night than think of such things.

"I thought you'd say that. So I brought you an apple." She held it out. "I've enchanted it so that a single bite will give you a night of dreamless sleep. Even a man of your size."

He took the apple, thanking her for the gift as he tucked it away for later. Much later, when they had reached Castrum, and he could finally sleep soundly.

If they reached Castrum.

Xylander waited for Guinevere to fall asleep before he banked the fire, hiding its light so that no one would see them from the road. She'd taken such good care of him after their mother died – it was time he repaid the favour.

Three

They arrived at Castrum in the late afternoon, not long before the city gates closed at sunset. Xylander insisted on sleeping the night at an inn before entering Artorius' court, and Guinevere was grateful. A bath and a bed for the night after such a wearying journey was just what she needed.

The sounds of the city woke her at dawn, and she had never been one to lie abed when there was work to be done. She unbraided her hair, still slightly damp from its washing last night, and combed it until it was dry. Without a maid to help her and only her blurred reflection in the scratched bronze mirror to guide her, Guinevere knew better than to attempt to dress her own hair as would be expected at her father's court.

She changed into a fresh shift, then laid out her dresses to see if anything would suit. She'd rolled them all together in the saddlebag, so the silks and linens were now hopelessly creased, but the one woollen gown she'd tightly rolled in the heart of the bundle had not suffered the same fate. The white lambswool smoothed out at a touch, its softness strange under her fingers after so long wearing rough squire's clothes.

"By all that's holy, Guin, put some clothes on. You're haloed against the firelight, and though you might look heaven-sent to any other man like that, heaven knows I don't want to see my sister naked."

The sight of Xylander with an arm thrown over his eyes, as if to block out the morning light, brought laughter to her lips as it lightened her heart. She slipped the white gown over her head as she said, "So you think King Artorius will be willing to marry me?"

"Any man would be willing to marry you," Xylander said. "Except me, of course."

"Of course." She tied her laces, then adjusted her girdle so it sat right. "Do I look good enough for court, Lander?"

"If there is a man among them who dares say otherwise, I shall challenge them on the spot," he said, filling the basin with water and dunking his head in. He came up spluttering. "And fight for your honour."

She snorted. "What good would it do for you to get stuck on a sword?"

He drew himself up haughtily. "I am an expert swordsman. In the battle for your honour, it will be the other man who is pierced by my blade."

"Even worse. I'm sure Artorius will really want to marry me, knowing it's my fault one of his knights was slayed for simply slighting me."

Xylander rubbed his face vigorously with a towel, then blinked at her. "A truly noble king would recognise the loyalty you command in your men, and be even more eager for an alliance."

"Do you think Father will honour such an alliance?"

Xylander's wince answered for him.

They ate a silent breakfast, and all too soon made their way up the spiralling streets to the castle.

Four

At this early hour, Father's court would have been empty, but King Artorius evidently rose early, and everyone knew it. Xylander wished he'd known it, as he craned his neck over the crowd to the throne on the dais. Yes, there was a man sitting on it, who surely must be the king.

"All of the women wear veils here!" Guinevere hissed, looking stricken.

Xylander shrugged. What did it matter if she covered her hair or not?

The party of merchants currently petitioning

the King bowed and moved out of the way.

Xylander straightened. There they were –
Artorius' famous knights. Each clad in a
different surcoat, emblazoned with the
symbols that were as legendary as the men
themselves. He'd heard they stood as equals in
Artorius' court, but every group had a leader,
the first among equals, and the first among
them was the man wearing an azure surcoat,
emblazoned with a sword in either silver or
white – it was hard to tell at this distance.

"I'll go speak to the herald, so he can
announce you," Xylander said, squeezing
inside the crowded hall. He might not be
dressed in his princely best, but the sword on
his hip proclaimed he was wealthier than most
of the peasants hoping to be heard today, and
the crowd parted for him.

He took his time scanning the court, taking
in as much as he could, before giving
Guinevere's name to the herald. Then he
hurried back to her.

"The King is old, older than Father," he
murmured in her ear. "Guin, I don't think he
wants a bride. We may have to go somewhere

else."

"Where would you have me go? No, Lander, Castrum is strong enough to withstand an attack, even from Father's armies. I'm not leaving here." From the set of her chin, he knew it would be futile arguing with her.

An idea came to him. "If he refuses you, ask to marry one of his knights. They are all of noble blood, and any one of them will protect you with his life." Xylander grasped her arm. "You will be much happier with some handsome knight than a white-haired old king, Guin."

She shook him off. "Don't be daft. Father betrothed me to the King, or tried to, and I will honour his offer. Just because a man is handsome doesn't make him a good husband."

Xylander tried again. "Yes, but – "

"Her Royal Highness, Princess Guinevere of Flamand," the herald boomed.

Xylander's heart sank.

Five

Guinevere heard her name, but the roaring in her ears blocked out everything else. A path opened up before her, walled with people on either side, and she marched forward, her head held high.

Every woman wore a veil – she was the only one with her head uncovered. And why had she chosen to wear white? Artorius' court all wore dark, sombre colours, making her look as out of place as snow in summer.

Yet the wall of humanity wilted as she passed – bows and curtseys, as one would expect for a princess. The only ones who remained standing were a crowd of men off to the side of the King's dais. They looked like knights tricked out for a tourney, with their brightly coloured surcoats. Every one of them stared avidly at her.

She did her best to ignore them, and curtseyed deeply at the foot of the King's dais.

"Princess Guinevere of Flamand. What brings you to Castrum?"

She looked up, fixing her eyes on the King's bushy, white, raised eyebrows. "I have come to offer myself in marriage, to forge an alliance between our two countries."

The eyebrows bunched, almost meeting in the middle. "I told your father I have no need for another bride. I will send you home with an honour guard." He motioned toward the knights. "Lancelot, assemble a squad of your best men. You shall escort the princess home to Flamand, and you shall tell King Ludgar – "

"No." Guinevere held up her hand to stop the King, and found she had stopped the bright blue knight, too, whose sword-emblazoned surcoat stood mere inches from her hand. She met the knight's eyes, and was surprised to find they matched his surcoat, despite his dark hair.

A knight in her father's court would have ducked his head instantly, knowing he was not worthy to read the princess's soul, but this knight held her gaze with a mix of curiosity and approval.

You will be much happier with some handsome knight, the memory of her brother's voice whispered.

He was so handsome, just looking at him made her heart sing, this blue knight. But no amount of singing would keep her safe. Only the King could do that.

"No, King Artorius. I did not undertake the perilous journey from my father's kingdom to yours only to fail in my quest now. My father does not forgive failure. No matter how many knights you send, they will not be able to protect me from my father's wrath. I am a dutiful daughter, and I will be wed." Or she had been a dutiful daughter until now. Damn Father for driving her to this. A tear slipped down her cheek, and her voice dropped to a whisper. "Please, Your Majesty, do not send me back."

Silence fell, before the whispering began. Guinevere held the King's gaze, letting her eyes speak for her. Help me, please.

"Come, Princess." Artorius extended a hand toward her, palm up, while he waved away the blue knight with the other. "Come and sit beside me."

She grasped the King's hand, and rose. He guided her to the throne beside his – the queen's throne – and made her sit.

Then he called for the next petitioner.

Numbly, Guinevere sat beside him, only half listening to the endless stream of petitions and the judgements Artorius made. The words washed over her, but some things she did notice.

Unlike her father, Artorius never raised his voice, or lost his temper.

The blue knight never took his eyes off her.

And at the end of the audience, when Artorius rose to dismiss his court, he still kept hold of her hand.

"Three days' hence, there will be a

celebratory feast, to mark the marriage of two kingdoms, when I will take Princess Guinevere as my bride," Artorius announced.

Guinevere almost cried with relief, but managed to restrain herself, for she felt everyone's eyes upon her.

Everyone but the blue knight, who suddenly found the flagstones at his feet far more fascinating.

Six

Xylander headed back to the inn, thinking to collect his things and ride away. Now Guinevere was safe, he could be on his way. Find his own destiny, so to speak, as far from his father as possible.

"Is she fair, the princess?"

"The fairest lady I have ever seen. Skin white as fresh-fallen snow, lips as red as blood…"

Xylander grinned. Guinevere didn't think she had any beauty to speak of, but she'd turned every head in court today, male and female alike. She'd been wasted, shut up in Father's castle. Here, she would be allowed to bloom.

Or at least he hoped so. Perhaps he should stay for a little while, just to see how her marriage suited her. He owed her that.

"…and hair as black as ebony. The prettiest princess you ever saw, with a heart so soft, she covers her face and weeps at the sight of blood."

They weren't talking about Guinevere. Xylander had seen his sister hawking with their mother, and when her falcon had brought her a duck or a fat pigeon, she'd snapped their necks like any born hunter. Quick, decisive, yet without cruelty or enjoyment, heedless of the blood on her hands from the wounds the falcon's talons had gouged in her prey.

Even on the day Mother's gyrfalcon, Circe, had sliced through Mother's glove and drawn blood, Guinevere had held her head high, taking the bird from Mother before cleaning and bandaging Mother's arm. He'd wished for Guinevere, the first – and last – time he'd come to Castrum.

A time best forgotten.

"When she takes her place as queen, then we will truly know peace."

Xylander choked back a laugh. A leader who could not stand the sight of blood would not be strong enough to maintain any kind of peace.

"You dare laugh at our future queen?" a cool voice demanded.

Xylander blinked, realising the merchant was addressing him. Evidently he hadn't choked back his laughter soon enough. "It takes a strong leader to ensure peace. One like King Artorius. He's taking a new wife soon, who may yet give him a son. If she does, the princess will never be queen."

The merchant shook his head pityingly. "You know little of our king, sir. He has not taken another wife because he means to see Princess Zurine inherit his throne. The only son he wants is a son in law, a fitting consort for the princess, but no man is good enough."

Xylander opened his mouth to say that Artorius had thought he was good enough, then snapped it shut again. He was pretending to be a knight, not a prince. And he did not want their ebon-haired princess, who would never want to come hunting with him. He imagined her as a dark raincloud, raining tears too often.

Instead, he said, "The new queen is fair. Fair of eye and hair and skin...why, it might be said she is fairer than Princess Zurine. With a wife so fair, surely the King will not be able to resist begetting a son. Several, maybe."

One man slammed his empty cup down on the table. "Princess Zurine is the fairest maiden in the land, and I will fight any man who says otherwise!"

Xylander reached for his sword. "Princess Guinevere is fairer, and I will answer such an insult with my blade!"

He had barely a moment to think that perhaps Castrum was worth staying in, after all, if it was to be this much fun, before the brawl began in earnest and he found himself in the middle of the best fight he'd had in years.

Seven

"The white silk. His Majesty commands it."

The whirl of activity around Guinevere ceased, and the maids fell silent. Judging by the quality of her dress, the noblewoman who spoke of silk was some relation to the King.

But Guinevere had been her father's chatelaine for too many years to be cowed by a commanding tone, and here she would be queen. "White silk is impractical, and nothing like I saw the women wearing in court. Something darker would be much more sensible."

"The King commands that his bride will be wed in white. His queen will stand out in court, no matter what she wears, for you will sit beside him." The woman's stubborn chin jutted out as she matched Guinevere's gaze, then bobbed the slightest bit in a mocking curtsey. "Your Highness."

"Yes, Lady Ragna," the maids chorused. The maids bustled about her with the white silk, ignoring Guinevere's quiet protests.

"Your veil will be embroidered with gold thread, the same shade as your hair," Lady Ragna continued. "I will see to it myself." And with that, she turned in a swirl of skirts, and was gone, but for the clinking of the keyring at her girdle as she marched down the corridor.

The castle chatelaine, Guinevere guessed. One who already grasped the reins of the household firmly in hand. With such a woman already here, perhaps Guinevere could sit around in white silk, embroidering handkerchiefs or whatever took her fancy, for she would have little else to do. A situation as alien to her as the surface of the moon, for even when her mother was alive, Guinevere had been learning how to keep a castle. For, her mother had often said, a king might rule a kingdom, but it was the queen who ruled the castle, and to do that, she must know everything that went on within it, to make sure it ran as smoothly as possible. Yet Castrum coped fine without a queen.

Castrum was shaping up to be a very different place to home, she reflected. She wasn't sure if that was a good thing, or a bad one.

Then again, in her two days in Castrum, no one had shouted at her, threatened to kill her, or brought her an impossible problem and begged her to solve it.

Perhaps she could learn to like it here. White silk, idleness and all.

Eight

The wedding was a mercifully brief affair, so unmemorable that even after, as she sat on the queen's throne beside Artorius in court, nodding her gratitude for the endless stream of wedding gifts being presented by his vassals, the only details she could recall were about the cathedral. Older than the one at home, an altar before which they'd said their vows sat beneath a circular dome that appeared to be a giant caricature of the bishop's bald head below it.

Firmly yet with great courtesy, Artorius took

her hand to guide her from cathedral to throne room, and then on to the feasting hall, where he seated her beside him on the dais. A girl close to her own age sank onto the bench beside Guinevere. A girl who wore white silk, just like her. Guinevere opened her mouth to greet the girl.

"Princess, you have not yet congratulated your father and his new bride," said a male voice from the girl's other side.

Guinevere found herself impaled by the girl's gimlet glare, as the girl pursed her lips into a disapproving rosebud. "She's wearing my silk. I can't help but wonder what else she means to usurp while she's here. I can't imagine what my father was thinking."

The man leaned forward, his eyes bulging as they avidly regarded Guinevere.

She'd never minded people staring at her before, but the touch of this man's eyes made her skin crawl. She wanted to bathe all over again, scrubbing fiercely until she could no longer feel it.

His tongue darted out, licking plump lips. "He was thinking like a man. A man with needs that must be met. Needs that only a wife can truly satisfy. I'm sure when you are a wife, you will understand. If you had but accepted my offer, tonight could have been a double celebration, and I would only be too happy to educate you in all your wifely duties. Just say the word, Princess."

Though the lecherous man spoke to the princess, his eyes were undressing Guinevere.

Like Artorius would, after the feast, in the privacy of his bedchamber.

Her wedding night. Guinevere shivered. She had heard many tales about what happened, both bad and good, and she prayed she would not embarrass herself or her new husband. That would be enough. To hope for the pleasure she'd heard some women experienced in the bedchamber…no, that was too much to hope for.

"Lord Melwas, I would not marry you if you were the last man on earth. My father has promised I shall marry a prince, and I am content to wait until he comes to claim me. On that day, I will celebrate." The girl drank deeply from her wine.

Guinevere smothered a laugh. Artorius' daughter might not like her, but she quite liked the daughter. Guinevere vowed to help the girl marry her prince, if that's what she wanted. Perhaps the girl might come to like her, if she could arrange it.

Nine

As a mere knight, Xylander sat far to the back of the hall, where the men ate off trenchers instead of plates. Not that he minded the plain fare – he'd eaten plenty such on hunting trips. As long as there was plenty of it, and there was. King Artorius kept a good table.

Up at the high table, Guinevere sat like a marble statue come to life. Her veil hid her golden hair, but he'd know his sister anywhere. She was born to be a queen.

The men around him toasted the health of their new queen, and the King, until they toasted more for another drink than whatever they were well-wishing. Xylander downed his drink, and decided to risk it. Artorius was busy talking to the man beside him, so Xylander could pretend to be as drunk as his fellows and approach the dais to wish the couple well. The King would likely ignore him, as he should to some drunken junior knight, but Guinevere would appreciate it, and she was the one who mattered.

Xylander wove between tables, revellers and servers, his eyes fixed on Guinevere. She caught sight of him and flashed a smile that spoke more of hope than happiness. A hope for happiness, perhaps.

He should have been watching where he was going.

He smacked into someone, nearly knocking the slight figure down. He reached out to steady her, and found his hands ensnared in silk.

Only then did he drag his eyes from Guinevere to meet…hers.

Dark eyes peered up at him, shocked.

Xylander ducked his head, praying she

would not recognise him, if she hadn't yet already. If she knew him as the Green Knight, he'd be dead for sure. "Please forgive me, sweet lady." He bowed low.

She made a disapproving sound deep in her throat. In a rustle of silk, she was gone.

Xylander dared to breathe again, only to inhale her dizzying scent. Something sweet and floral, enchanting him even more.

Rough hands seized his arms as a red-faced courtier took her place before him. "How dare you touch the princess!" the courtier hissed.

He'd hoped to find her a gorgon, but her beauty had bloomed since he'd seen her last. Princess Zurine was as beauteous as Guinevere, if not more.

It mattered not. She'd seen his hideous defeat in that tourney, years ago, and wouldn't want anything to do with him.

Better that he leave. Now. Before she remembered, and sent more guards after him than these two. Xylander twisted out of their hold and hurried out of the hall.

Ten

"Come, wife, it is time to take you to my chamber," Guinevere heard Artorius say, and his hand engulfed hers.

She wiped her lips to hide their trembling, then let the cloth fall as Artorius led her away from the high table.

Guinevere held her head high, as a queen should, marching with firm steps behind her new king, hoping no one could see the tumult inside. The sheer terror at what was to come.

Someone fell into step behind her. She glanced back, hoping to meet Xylander's gaze so that the eye contact might bolster her courage, but she found one of Artorius' knights following her instead. The knight bowed his head rather than meet her eyes, but it didn't stop her from recognising him. This was the azure knight who'd stared at her so when she first entered Artorius' court. Up close and in his wedding finery, he cut an even finer figure than before.

For one mad, glorious moment, she wished she could have married the handsome knight instead of his king, so that her wedding night might feel like more of a pleasure than a duty. But a lone knight could not protect her from her father's forces, if her father came after her, while King Artorius could command armies of strong knights.

The price of protection was to share the King's bed. A price she had promised to pay, and she would.

"Your chamber, my queen," King Artorius said, opening a door and ushering her inside.

He did not miss her hesitation.

He clapped a hand on the knight's shoulder. "This is Sir Lancelot, the most loyal of my knights. There is no man I trust more to guard the door of my chamber, or yours."

Lancelot dropped to one knee, accepting her hand from his king. "I am honoured, Your Majesties." His lips touched the back of Guinevere's hand.

She gasped as lightning seemed to spark at his touch, running up her arm into the very heart of her. She darted a frightened glance at the King, hoping he hadn't seen.

But of course he had, for he watched her closely.

"You have nothing to fear while Sir Lancelot protects you, my queen," Artorius said. "Now, step inside, while I have a word with him."

She had no choice but to obey her husband, no matter how much she felt the urge to run. A foolish urge, she told herself, as she entered the royal bedchamber. She spied the chest that was evidently used to store their crowns and breathed a sigh of relief. Never had something weighed her down as much as the circlet of gold atop her head, and she felt so much lighter as she laid the queen's crown in its proper place. She must have unfastened the fillet that held her veil in place, too, for she felt the fabric slide down her back into a pile on the floor.

She nudged the richly embroidered cloth with her slippered foot. Hours of work had gone into every stitch, in anticipation of this day, and now the day was over, she had no desire to take it up again.

She heard a gasp, and turned, to find both Sir Lancelot and King Artorius staring at her.

Lancelot ducked his head. "To my last breath, Your Majesty."

Another clap to the knight's shoulder. "Good boy."

From the furrow in the knight's brow, Guinevere judged he did not agree with his sovereign, but he had the grace not to say so. She wouldn't have called Lancelot a boy, either – he was most definitely a man – yet she had no desire to argue with her new husband.

She would struggle enough to be meek and compliant. By all that was holy, why had she agreed to –

The door clicked shut, and Artorius

slammed the bar into place, barring the chamber to all but themselves.

There would be no escape now. Guinevere swallowed back her terror. It had no place here.

The King smiled. "Your hair is like spun gold. You will need to cover it in court, or you will blind my men with your beauty."

She bobbed a curtsey. "Yes, Your Majesty." For all she'd been taught about protocol and the proper things a wife did for her husband, she could not for the life of her remember how she was supposed to address him.

He dropped his crown into the chest. "Artorius, please. Or just Art, if you wish. Titles are for court or the battlefield, and you have no need to be present at either, if you do not wish it. Truly, I am too old to be breaking in a new wife, but I could never refuse aid to a damsel in distress. Now we are alone, tell me truly, Guinevere: is this the fate you would have chosen?"

Better than the alternative. "Yes, Your...Artorius."

He chuckled, but his shrewd, old eyes saw

too much. "Or at least you fear me less than your father."

"I do not fear you." Damn his eyes. "I fear...what all new brides do, is all." She ducked her head so that she might unlace her gown without him reading her very soul.

"And rightly so, perhaps. A young man faced with a beautiful woman forgets himself and what is due to his bride, far too often." He glanced at the door, perhaps thinking of Lancelot. "A wedding night is only properly consummated when both parties are willing and ready to join together in every way. I will not ask anything of you unless you are ready, Guinevere."

Her gown puddled around her ankles, but the laces on her shift had somehow tied themselves into impossible knots. She dragged the garment up over her head and threw it on the floor. "I am ready." Ignoring how the cool air chilled her skin, she marched to the bed and lay down, closing her eyes tightly. "I am ready," she repeated, as much to herself as to him.

She felt his weight as he climbed into the

bed beside her.

She squeezed her eyes shut tighter, trying to visualise the handsome knight naked. She would imagine he was Lancelot, and the ordeal would be over soon.

"Well, I am not," Artorius said. "Drinking all those toasts to our health and happiness, I fear has given me a splitting headache. One that cannot be cured even by the sight of your beautiful body. So cover yourself, my dear, and get some sleep. I certainly intend to."

By all that was holy, no. He could not do this to her. She had the courage for this now, but tomorrow...or another night...who knew if she could summon such courage again?

"But if the marriage is not consummated..." she began.

He cut her off with a loud snore.

Guinevere's eyes flew open. The snoring continued. Her husband had fallen asleep, without laying a finger on her.

She waited until she was certain he wouldn't wake before she slid beneath the blankets. Obedient wife that she was, she tried to sleep.

Eleven

Guinevere couldn't say what woke her, but as her sleep-fogged mind registered the heavy breathing in the bed beside her, the weight of dread pulled her out from under the covers. The room still held the warmth of last night's fire, now little more than ashes in the hearth she edged toward, but a chill settled over her as she reached for a shift to clothe her nakedness.

The white silk gown, puddled where it had fallen, reminded her that she was a new bride, and her heavy-breathing bedmate was her husband, but it couldn't dim her desire to dress before he woke. Only when she'd laced up her lavender linen gown did she dare to approach the bed again on slippered feet.

Artorius' eyes opened, but they filled with horror at the sight of her.

Guinevere wet her lips. "It is I, Guinevere, your new queen," she said.

He flopped like a landed fish, one arm pounding the mattress while the other hung, lifeless, over the edge of the bed. He made a hoarse sound, but there were no words in it.

And his face…why, it almost looked like it had drooped, all down one side…

Apoplexy, Guinevere's mind told her, as her horrified eyes met his. Just like Mother, who had died the day this happened to her.

But Artorius couldn't die. He was her husband, he'd promised to protect her. If he died, she'd have to go back home to her father's wrath…or worse, run again.

In desperation, she did the only thing she could do. She bit her lip and cast a sleeping spell on the King. A spell strong enough to stop the illness from progressing, or at least slow it, yet it put him into a slumber light enough that he still drew breath and appeared to sleep naturally.

Outside her chamber, she found the guard had changed, so she did not need to meet the eyes of the handsome man who'd made her heart flutter last night. Instead the new guard bowed deeply. "Your Majesty."

She nodded in acknowledgement and tried to step past him.

"How fares the King?"

She stopped. "He…sleeps still. Last night, he…was tired, and drank a lot of wine."

The knight nodded and moved aside.

Guinevere considered telling him that the King was not well, but to say the words aloud was to make the King's fate unavoidable. No, she could not tell him. Let the knight find him, and a healer who could work miracles that might save him. To lose her husband like she'd lost her mother was a cruel twist of fate she could not bear.

It was early yet, so instead of going to the Great Hall, she headed for the kitchen in search of something with which to break her fast.

She followed the yeasty scent of baking bread to the kitchen, then stood in the doorway, admiring the purpose-filled bustle below. In a well-run kitchen such as this, the chatelaine would have little waste to worry about. Why, looking around, you would not guess that a huge feast had been prepared here only yesterday.

"Your Majesty?"

Lady Ragna's voice was unmistakeable.

"The King and his daughter prefer to take breakfast in the Great Hall. If you tell me what you wish to eat, I shall see that it is brought up to you."

Every head turned to stare at her then, before the entire kitchen staff sank into deep curtseys.

Her appearance had never stopped all work in the kitchen at home, Guinevere thought wryly. "I will have...whatever the others normally have," she said.

"Very good, Your Majesty," said Lady Ragna.

Guinevere half expected the woman to pat

her on the head, like her nurse had when she was a child.

"If you have lost your way, I can show you to the Great Hall," Lady Ragna continued, gesturing.

Of course. The kitchen staff still hadn't moved. "Please," Guinevere agreed.

"Along that passage way, turn right, then follow that to the end, and you shall be in the Great Hall," Lady Ragna said, edging between Guinevere and the kitchen. Blocking her way, leaving her no choice but to leave.

Guinevere got the message, all right. She might be queen, but Lady Ragna ran the castle. There was no place for a queen in the kitchen.

Twelve

"Mark my words, cousin. If your father rises from his bed today, it will be a miracle indeed."

Guinevere recognised the sneering voice of the man who'd been sitting beside the princess last night. Instead of continuing into the Great Hall, she retreated down the corridor, where the shadows would hide her from sight while she could still listen.

"If you have poisoned my father, Lord Melwas, I will see you tried and executed for treason. He will rise as readily as he has every other morning."

That was the princess.

Guinevere's blood ran cold. What did Melwas know about the King's condition? Could the man have poisoned his king somehow? But how would he have known to give him a poison to make his death look like Mother's?

"Oh, not me, dear cousin. I would not dream of poisoning the King. That little slut who seduced him into yesterday's farce of a marriage might, though. Probably already pregnant with some other man's bastard, she came here to seduce your father, meaning to set her bastard son upon the throne, and act as regent until the boy is of age. For after spending a night with your father, then silencing him before the night is over, who could say that her child is not his?"

"She is pregnant? How do you know?" the princess asked, sounding wistful.

"The woman walked into court with her hair uncovered. You were not there, so you did not see, but ask any lady of the court who was. She walked in with her hair as loose as the devil's own snares, as brazen as the lord of hell himself. Only virtuous women wear veils, like your good self. Mark my words, cousin, the King may have laid a crown on the little whore's head, but no mere metal can make her fit to be queen."

"What can we do?"

"We are strongest together, cousin. You are his only child, and I am his closest male heir. If anything happens to your father, we must marry, for only when we are united can we keep the throne from that slut of a usurper."

The princess made a disgusted sound. "I should have known you are full of wind and little else, Lord Melwas. When my father comes to break his fast, proving you wrong, I will tell him of your silly stories, and your relentless quest for my hand, and he will put an end to them both. Perhaps he will send you to inspect the salt mines on the eastern border...for those lands are yours, are they not? You spend so much time at court, it is difficult to remember you have a home of your own."

"You're a fool, Zurine. Once your father is dead, she will come after you."

"But if you are so sure you are Father's heir, surely she would come after you first?"

This time the disgusted sound came from Melwas. "The slut is no match for me, and even she knows that, if you do not. She will choose the easier targets – you and your father – first, and wait for her father's armies to arrive before she even thinks to take me on. I could protect you...but only if you marry me."

"I'll take my chances, Lord Melwas, and I will take my breakfast alone in my chambers. Talking to you makes me lose my appetite every time."

Princess Zurine's footsteps approached. Guinevere sank deeper into the shadows, praying the girl would not see her.

Thirteen

"Is there a knight called Sir Lander staying here?"

All heads in the taproom turned toward the guard who'd spoken, but no one answered.

"He is needed up at the castle," the guard continued, growing impatient.

Tense shoulders relaxed, and most of the men resumed drinking. All but Xylander, who debated whether to answer the summons or flee.

If it were his father's summons, fleeing would be the wiser choice. But this was

Castrum, not home, and this king had showed no signs of madness.

"What's he needed for?" Xylander called.

Now heads turned toward him, out of curiosity more than anything else. In Flamand, dread would have elicited sharp gasps from the men, as they hunched their shoulders in relief that the curse of the King's notice had passed them by…but mad kings were mercifully absent in this kingdom.

Xylander rose to his feet and repeated, "Why does the castle need Sir Lander?"

The guard coughed. "She did not say."

Xylander's heart soared. The princess had discovered his name, and summoned him. Of course she would not tell a mere guard what she wanted. Perhaps she had recognised him from before. Had her thoughts been filled with him, like his dreams last night had been haunted by her?

"Perhaps she'll tell me, then," he said. "For I am Sir Lander." He fastened his cloak and followed the guard out.

One guard, who made no move to restrain him. This was an invitation, and a polite one, at that. He was indeed needed. Perhaps wanted, too.

People bustled about, paying him no heed as they passed him in the castle corridors. Xylander was led ever upward, to where the royal family's apartments lay, he was certain.

Surely he had not made that much of an impression on the princess that she'd summoned him to her bedchamber.

Yet if he had…

The guard knocked on a door. "Sir Lander, mistress," he said, sweeping the door open and gesturing for Xylander to enter.

Xylander stepped inside.

Fourteen

"Finally!" Guinevere stopped pacing at the sight of her brother. "Shut the door."

Xylander did, looking confused.

She didn't give him a chance to ask questions. Not until she'd told him everything, when she was sure he'd have questions aplenty.

"The King took ill last night. Like…like Mother did, on the day she died." Tears itched at the corners of her eyes, but Guinevere drew in a deep breath and blinked them away. "I put him into a healing sleep, but that will only delay the end. Unless some miracle occurs, he will die, and that will leave us worse off than before."

Xylander nodded.

"The succession here after his death is…not so clear. He has one daughter, Princess Zurine. Old enough to marry, but as yet unwed. His closest male relation is Lord Melwas, a courtier of considerable power who seeks to cement that by marrying the princess. If he does, he will become king." Guinevere sucked in another breath. "I heard them talking today. They believe I have come here on Father's orders to kill them all. The King, the princess…all of them, then claim the throne for myself."

Xylander opened his mouth, likely to utter a horrified protest.

"They won't let us stay here, Lander. They'll send us home, unless we can find a way to prevent it. Prevent Melwas from becoming the next king."

"You want me to kill Lord Melwas, then?" Xylander asked. He thought for a moment, then rubbed his hands together. "It will be a simple matter. I shall call him out for speaking ill of the Queen, and when I am victorious, you will be safe. I've sworn to protect you, and if it means killing a man, so be it."

If only it were so simple.

"No. I need you to…take the princess out of the picture." He would say no for certain, but she had to try.

"You want me to do what to the princess?"

She hushed him. If anyone heard him, word might get back to Melwas that what he'd suspected was true. "I want you to…" Seduce the girl, so she fell in love with Xylander and married him instead of Melwas. Reveal to the princess that he was the prince she longed for, and claim the King's crown.

Things Xylander would never agree to, even if it was the only way they could stay here. He wanted to fight and hunt and never take up his royal duties. As for seducing anyone, he would consider it beneath his honour to do such a thing. How could she word it so he would not refuse?

"Think of it like a quest. A hunt, if you will, for a pure and elusive creature, who you alone must conquer. You must capture her heart, or all will be lost."

Xylander's eyes widened in surprise. "You want her heart?"

It sounded so crude, put like that, but how else could she say it? "Only if her heart is in your possession, yours and yours alone, will we be able to stay here. You promised to keep me safe, Lander. This is the only way."

He swallowed. "I made an oath, and I shall keep it, though it will cost me dearly. It will be as you wish. May heaven forgive me."

Fifteen

Guinevere wanted him to kill the princess. Xylander didn't want to believe it, but she would never lie to him about something so serious.

So, no matter what his feelings were for the lovely princess, he would honour his oath to Guinevere. Because family and honour meant far more than some pretty maiden, princess or no.

He would do this one thing for her, then leave Castrum.

For with the princess dead, he would have

nothing to keep him here.

Sixteen

Guinevere took her dinner alone in her chamber, not sure she could face Lord Melwas and his suspicions again. To have come so far, and think she was finally safe, only to be cast into a pit of uncertainty again…fate must truly hate her.

"Beg pardon, Your Majesty…" The guard bowed from the doorway.

Guinevere dropped her spoon back into her half-eaten bowl of soup. She had no appetite today, anyway. "Yes?"

"Your presence is required in the throne

room."

Was the queen expected to dispense justice in the absence of the king? She had little experience in such things, but she would do her duty, if she must.

She rose and followed the guard.

Heavens, did she look queenly enough to sit in judgement?

She'd never had to worry much about her appearance back home – the maids had obeyed her orders whether she appeared immaculate or covered in dust with straw in her hair.

Well, she hadn't touched any straw today, so a quick pat told her that her hair was fine. A glance down her front confirmed that she hadn't spilled her soup. The lacings on her bodice sat straight and firmly tied, though she tugged on them just to make sure. And her slippers were so new, she could scarcely feel the flagstones beneath her feet, so there could be no holes.

Did she need her crown?

She almost turned back to get it, then remembered that it was in the bedchamber she'd shared with Artorius. Where he slept still.

He had not worn a crown on the day she'd petitioned him. Even if he had, her mother had said many times that a lady of royal blood needed no such thing to proclaim her authority – everyone should know she was a queen by the way she entered a room, or walked through it.

Crownless, she would make her mother proud.

Guinevere drew herself up, lifting her chin as she straightened her shoulders, looking ahead instead of at the flagstones.

When she reached the throne room, she swept in, not waiting to be announced. She reigned here, second only to the King himself, who was not here.

The crowd of courtiers parted before her, a sea of bows and curtseys showing her the way to her throne.

One man stood in her way: Sir Lancelot.

He met her gaze for only a moment before bowing deeply, like the rest, but as he stood on the dais steps, even bent over, he stood higher than she.

"Your Majesty. We feared that the illness

which has struck down the King might have affected you, too, but by some miracle, you are well. We must be thankful for small mercies."

So they knew about the King's illness. She wasn't sure whether his words were meant to trap her into an incriminating response, or if he genuinely meant what he said. His emotionless gaze gave away nothing.

Guinevere merely nodded once and ascended to her throne.

Lancelot hushed the ill wind of whispering with one hand.

"Your Majesty, lords and ladies of the court, good knights, some of whom have already heard our ill news. The King's illness was both sudden and unexpected, and has kept him to his bed today. Our best healers are with him, and doing everything within their power to see him well again."

"It's her fault!"

Guinevere found a pudgy man pointing his finger at her. The other courtiers edged away from him, and she realised this was Lord Melwas.

"Keep her away from the King or worse will

happen!"

Lancelot put up two placatory hands. "Of course, Her Majesty cannot sleep in a sick chamber. A new bride who may well be in a delicate condition should be protected at all costs. We cannot have the Queen and any heir she might be carrying fall ill, too. The King would never forgive us."

Melwas looked like he had more to say, but he subsided. Nevertheless, Guinevere still felt his eyes upon her, as Lancelot dealt with any urgent matters that could not wait on the King's health.

He was as just as the King, declaring his judgement before deferring to her. A nod seemed to suffice, so she did not have to judge cases or say a word the whole time she sat there, yet justice was served, all the same.

Eventually, she began to tire, or perhaps it was boredom weighing down her eyelids, but the thought had barely crossed her mind before Lancelot declared the day's audience at an end.

The crowd dispersed, until only she and Lancelot remained.

He bowed before the dais. "I hope my presumption did not displease you, my queen. It was I who sent the guard to get you, when Lord Melwas summoned the court. If I had not, I fear he would have declared his regency until the King is well again. With you present, he did not dare."

Guinevere managed a smile. "When the King is well again, I am certain he will be grateful for your care for his kingdom."

His eyes met hers, sadness piercing her as surely as his gaze did. "Did you not hear, Your Majesty? It appears the King is gravely ill, and the healers fear he may not wake at all. Princess Zurine said she would tell you herself, and headed to your chamber to break the news. Did you not see her?"

Guinevere shook her head. Then a twist of dread tied her stomach in a knot. If Zurine had come while she was speaking to Xylander, and heard her...

"Strange," Lancelot said. "Perhaps Her Highness was so overcome by her father's illness that it slipped her mind. I shall speak to her. If Melwas summons the court again, it would be best if both you and the princess could be present. For in the absence of the King, the presence of the two women he loves most would reassure the populace."

Love? How could this knight talk of love between her and the husband she did not know? Would never know, now. Tears clouded Guinevere's eyes, and this time she could not drive them away. They trickled down her cheeks, twin testaments to her helplessness.

"I will see that Lady Ragna is made aware that you are to have your old chambers back. For the King will never forgive me if something were to happen to you."

The princess who'd run a whole castle, complete with its unpredictable king, now could not even control herself. Oh, how this knight must despise her.

But she was his queen, for all her weaknesses, and she must act like one.

Guinevere found her voice. "Thank you, Sir Lancelot," she said. Then she left, to find the safety of her chamber where she might weep in frustration without being watched.

Seventeen

Clouds had darkened the day early, so what had been a sunlit room when she left it yesterday was now a place of shadows and deeper darkness with the shutters closed. The newly lit fire didn't help matters, flickering weakly like a dying bird that had fallen down the chimney.

A fitting place for Queen Guinevere to sleep tonight, she grumbled to herself as she pushed the door shut behind her.

For the first time in her adult life, she wanted to throw herself on the floor and pound the flagstones until her frustration died. To be so close to safety and yet so far...

But if she did, the weariness already starting to weight her limbs would overcome her, and the floor was no place for a queen to sleep. Better that she take herself to bed instead, and pound the pillows without hurting her fists.

She took a step toward it, before the unfamiliar glitter stopped her.

"You need the help of a powerful man at court," said a voice that turned her stomach.

Melwas. The glitter of his eyes reminded her of a spider in the dark, only his eyes reflecting the firelight as he reclined on her bed.

Ugh. She wouldn't beat the pillows. She would burn them.

"But I am not the altruist that Artorius is, or was," Melwas continued smoothly. "A plea for help and a look from those big, sad eyes will not be enough to win me over. No, you will need to offer me something of value in exchange for helping you."

He rose from the bed, an ungainly manoeuvre that reminded her of a ballista ball being hefted out of a cartload of straw. A lot of rocking and rolling, puffing and blowing, until the man's feet finally touched the ground.

For all his girth, he stood no taller than her.

"I have nothing to offer you," Guinevere said. She meant it as a polite dismissal.

"That is not true," he said, taking a step toward her. "You have the jewels Artorius gave you as a wedding gift. Princess Zurine was furious when she discovered they were gone."

Jewels? The only item of jewellery Artorius had given her was a crown, and he had that still. Guinevere knew only a fool would hand this man a crown, even one fit for a queen.

"I might accept the jewels as a deposit. The first instalment of many," Melwas said. "Your father's kingdom has many treasures, so I am sure you have a fat dowry that Artorius will not miss."

Guinevere's mouth was too dry to speak. She could hardly tell this man that she'd fled Flamand with little more than a sack of clothing, and her father would probably disown her when he discovered what she'd done, if he hadn't already. She squeezed her eyes shut, not wanting to let this man see her cry.

He seized her, and when she opened her mouth to scream, he shoved his tongue down her throat, choking her. Thick lips bruised hers, as equally heavy hands kneaded her bottom like she was a loaf of bread he planned to devour.

A furious hammering sounded, somewhere far away.

Melwas released her, swearing, and she realised someone was knocking at the door. She sucked in a breath and called, "Come in!"

The door opened. Xylander spilled into the room, his eyes wild. "The princess is gone!"

"What did you say?" Melwas demanded.

Xylander stared at the man, as if he hadn't seen him before. "I said Princess Zurine has disappeared. No one has seen her all day. She's nowhere to be found in the castle."

Melwas swore, then hurried out.

Guinevere's legs could no longer hold her. She sat heavily on a chest, and let her tears fall. "I don't know what to do," she wept. Yet even as she said the words, her mind began making a list. "I need to change the bed, and send for water so that I can wash. Wine to wash out my mouth. Strong wine. Have a lock fitted to that door to which I have the only key..." She looked up to find Xylander staring at her. "You have to go after the girl. It doesn't matter if she's in the castle or if you have to chase her halfway to Flamand. Find her, Lander. Or I am doomed."

Xylander glanced back the way Melwas had gone, then looked at Guinevere. "Did he hurt you? I swore to defend you, and if he did anything, anything at all, I will slice him into pieces so small no one will know if the body is a man or a pig. I can't leave you here in danger. I swore an oath."

Oh, how much she longed to let him stay, to be her loyal bodyguard against that horrible excuse for a man.

But if anything happened to the princess...Melwas would be crowned king, and he could have whatever and whoever he wanted. Guinevere could not let that happen.

"He did nothing. I am upset about the King's illness and the missing princess," she insisted. "Find the girl. You know what to do."

Xylander looked pained, like he knew she lied. "Are you sure?"

Heaven help her, why did he tempt her so? Locks and a bath and fresh bedding would see her safe. It had to.

"Yes. And do not return until the girl's heart is yours," Guinevere said.

Eighteen

Tracking the princess took longer than Xylander expected. Perhaps because he was accustomed to tracking beasts in the forest, where there wasn't such a plethora of paths to follow, as there were outside the city gates. If he hadn't brought one of the palace hunting hounds and a pair of the princess's slippers with him, he suspected he would never have found the trail at all.

When her trail left the road to follow a track through the forest, Xylander sent the dog back to the palace and forged on alone.

The princess had evidently urged her horse to move swiftly, not an easy thing in the dense forest. A castle-bred girl who'd spent little time in the woods – if she hadn't wanted to be found, she should have kept to the road, where the steady stream of traffic might have hidden her tracks. Instead, she wandered through the forest, circling around one game trail before turning to another, with no clear direction in mind. Almost as if her heart hadn't truly been party to her sudden desire to run away.

Not like Guinevere, who had never looked back for a moment.

No, not like Guinevere at all.

Darkness had fallen by the time he found the princess, and he almost rode over the top of her in the dark.

A piercing scream ripped through the night, affrighting his horse so the mare reared and dumped Xylander unceremoniously on the ground before galloping off.

Xylander jumped to his feet, drawing his sword. "Show yourself!" he demanded.

She pulled off her hood, revealing her pale face. "Please do not hurt me, Sir Knight. Your horse frightened me as much as I frightened him."

"Her," Xylander corrected, sheathing his sword. "Like with people, I find female horses are better at doing what needs to be done than male ones. Except when it comes to war."

The girl shivered, pulling her cloak more closely about her. "I'm not sure if that's true. Why, I cannot even seem to start a fire." She waved at a pile of branches with no kindling or tinder in sight.

Xylander sighed. Why had Guinevere sent him out here to kill the girl? She would perish on her own of exposure without a fire. He could not bring himself to kill someone so helpless. It went against everything he believed in.

He would bring Guinevere the girl's heart, all right. But it would still be beating, locked in her breast. Oh, such a lovely, sweet breast.

All he had to do was persuade the girl to return to the castle where she belonged.

He held out his hand for her tinderbox. "Please, let me."

Nineteen

She wasn't hungry, but Guinevere forced down another bite of food without tasting it. She would need all her strength to get through the coming days.

"You cannot hide in your chamber forever. The people need to see their queen." Lady Ragna stood inside the room, voicing Guinevere's own thoughts, as she waved a procession of servants through the door.

One chest was deposited on the flagstones, the solid thump followed by twin relieved exhalations as the servants released their burdens. A second and third thump followed the first, before all six men bowed and departed.

Lady Ragna did not. "These are your court clothes, as the King commanded. In his absence, the people need their queen."

Guinevere stared at the chests. The clothes they contained could only be new, for she had not brought enough from Flamand to fill one chest, let alone three. She could not have commanded enough seamstresses in Flamand to do so much in so little time. "But it's only been a day," she said.

"A day in which you have been crowned queen, the King has been taken ill, and the princess has gone missing. If you mean to be queen for more than a day, you must take your place in the Great Hall and the throne room on the morrow. Or Lord Melwas will."

Lord Melwas. Who she could shut out while she stayed here, but she could not avoid if she had to leave her chamber. How one man could frighten her so, she wasn't sure, but Guinevere's hands shook at the very thought of him.

Lady Ragna pursed her lips. "I will send a maid up in the morning to help you dress for court. If you do not choose a suitable gown, then she will. You are part of King Artorius' family now, and while you might be more familiar with foreign ways, you will do things differently here. The King might be ill, but he will not be dishonoured by one such as you."

Ragna left without waiting for a response, which was probably just as well, for the words Guinevere wanted to say were certainly not queenly.

Anger forced her to her feet, and all the way to the door, where she considered shouting something after the bully of a chatelaine.

"Your Majesty."

Guinevere blinked as she met Lancelot's eyes before he bowed. Then he straightened again and faced the corridor, instead of her.

Like a guard, her bewildered mind supplied. He guarded her chamber, just as he'd guarded the royal bedchamber last night.

But no mere man could guard against death, which had stolen into the room and felled Artorius as he slept. Death would claim him in the end, for an enchanted sleep could only delay the inevitable.

She slammed the door and barred it, wanting to sink to her knees and cry, but this time, she knew she could not. Instead, she should busy herself…by examining the gowns Ragna had brought. Guinevere might not like the woman, but she agreed with her that a queen could not hide at dark times such as this. She would not dishonour Artorius, even if he would never know.

So she took stock of the gowns Ragna had brought, laying them one after the other on the bed that she'd had made up with fresh linen after Melwas' visit.

White linen and wool, edged in silk or a lovely golden fur she'd never seen at home. And the crown jewel of them all, a gold silk gown trimmed with white fur. Ermine, she thought. A gown fit for a queen that outshone even her wedding gown, which she had not yet found. Ah, she had only unpacked two chests so far – one stood untouched in the corner.

The final chest contained her wedding gown, as expected, but beneath it was a surfeit of underclothes, white as fresh snow. Stockings and shifts, veils that ranged from thickly woven wool to linen so fine she could see through it when she held it up to the light. And beneath it all sat two caskets she had not seen before.

She opened the first, and found it full of jewellery. Golden fillets, some jewelled and some plain, though she could hardly call such intricate workmanship plain. Gold lace, woven of fine metal wire instead of thread, formed a crown so light she would barely feel its weight when she wore it. There were necklaces, too, but the crown was a work of art.

She opened the next casket, expecting to see more of the same jewellery, but found it full of silver, not gold. A set of jewelled combs, and a set made of plain silver. And beneath those, a mirror, the like of which she'd never seen before.

This was a far cry from the scratched bronze in the inn. The silvery surface shone beneath a layer of some sort of crystal or glass – the biggest piece she'd ever seen, an oval bigger than her head. She'd never seen her own reflection so clearly – her skin so pale, making the dark, sleepless circles beneath her eyes stand out all the more.

What did her appearance matter? What she really wanted to see was her brother, successful in his mission.

As if on command, the mirror surface misted over for a moment, before clearing to show a forest in darkness.

Guinevere caught a flicker of movement, and peered closer.

"Here, let me," she heard Xylander say, as if he was in the room beside her.

The rasp of a flint, spitting sparks onto tinder, lit Princess Zurine's face for a moment before the girl pulled her cloak more closely about herself and backed away.

Someone hammered against the door. Guinevere almost dropped the mirror in surprise. "Who is it?" she called.

"Lord Melwas wishes to see you, Your Majesty."

Ugh. "Tell him I have no desire to see him," she called back.

"Open this door. I must see the Queen. It is

a private matter of great importance!" Melwas demanded.

She would rather die first. "I am indisposed. Return on the morrow."

The door rattled violently, and she heard Melwas swear. Thankfully, the bar she'd dropped across it held.

"You will regret this, Queen Guinevere!" he shouted.

She doubted it, but she didn't tell him that. Instead, she busied herself, returning her gowns to their places, except for a fawn-coloured one trimmed in white silk that seemed the most practical of them all. On the morrow, she would wear it to court, as she waited for Xylander to return with the princess. All would be well, she was certain of it.

Twenty

Zurine accepted the bread and cheese Xylander handed to her, though she was more hesitant about the skin of wine. He gulped down some wine, to show her it was safe, before she sipped from that, too.

"What is a lady like you doing in the woods? What are you running from?" he asked.

Zurine took a larger swallow of wine. "My stepmother's assassins."

Xylander choked.

Zurine managed a sickly smile. "I know it sounds silly. I said as much to my cousin, when he said she would try to kill me, but then I heard her. She was talking to someone – a man – and demanding he bring my heart to her to prove he'd done what she asked. I could not stay in my father's house with her after that. Just waiting for the axe to fall. So…I ran."

A foolish thing to do for a girl on her own, who had no idea how to survive in the woods. "Why didn't you ask someone for help? Find someone to protect you?" If she'd come to him first…

"My father might have, but he has fallen deathly ill. At my stepmother's hand, if my cousin is to be believed, and I am beginning to think he might be right."

Xylander shook his head. No. Guinevere would never have hurt her husband. Not when she relied upon his protection. "What about your cousin? Would he protect you?"

Zurine laughed weakly. "He says he can, but for a price. He wants to marry me, and claim my father's lands as his own. My father made other plans for me, but if he dies…I fear my prince may never come." She swiped her hands across her face. "You must think me a fool."

"No," Xylander lied. "I think you are very brave." That, at least, was true. To leave her father's castle for the unknown meant she had a great deal of courage. "But I think you would be wiser to seek shelter than to stay out here in the open. Perhaps an inn in the city…"

He stopped when he saw her shaking her head.

"In the city, someone will recognise me, and her assassins will find me. I cannot return."

Xylander's heart sank. Winning the girl's trust would take too long, and even then, she might still refuse to return to the city with him. He had to try something else.

He dug through the pouch at his belt and extracted an apple. The enchanted apple Guinevere had given him. If it put her to sleep, he could carry her back to the city before she woke.

"Here, an apple from my father's orchard. I'd be delighted to share it with you, Princess," he said, holding it out.

She eyed it suspiciously.

Xylander sighed. He'd have to eat some of

this, too. Just be careful not to swallow, lest he fall asleep, too. He took a bite, then handed the apple to her.

Zurine lifted it to her lips, her dark eyes regarding him.

He met her gaze, willing her to trust him, but the darkness in her eyes seemed to grow deeper, expanding until blackness engulfed him.

Twenty-One

Xylander woke slowly, revelling in how well-rested he felt. He could not recall how long it had been since he'd slept so well. Why, he could almost imagine himself in his own bed in his father's castle, he was so comfortable.

He opened his eyes, and realisation dawned. He wasn't home, nor in a bed, and the trees surrounding him seemed to mock him for his stupidity.

He'd eaten Guinevere's apple. There was still a piece in his mouth – he hadn't swallowed it. Yet it had enchanted him, all the same.

He spat it on the ground, cursing as he realised he was alone beside the ashes of a cold fire. No fire, no horse, and no Zurine, either. She'd even taken the rest of the bloody apple.

Something about the apple must have made her suspicious. Maybe she'd seen that he hadn't swallowed, or maybe she'd recognised him, after all. Ah, by all that was holy, what did it matter? The girl was gone and he had to find her again.

Swearing, he found fresh hoofprints and set off after them.

This time, she'd taken a relatively direct route back to the road, surprising him. Had she returned to the city, after all? Or headed away from it, taking the road away from everything she'd known, just as he and Guinevere had?

A rustling sound drew his attention to the roadside. A horse stepped delicately through the long grass, crunching her way through them.

The princess's horse, saddled and bridled, but missing her saddlebags.

And the princess herself was nowhere to be

seen.

Xylander swore again.

Guinevere would not be happy.

Then again, if the girl had slipped away from him, then she was safe. All he had to do was give Guinevere a heart and tell her it was the girl's and Guin would be satisfied.

Xylander headed back into the woods. He would hunt, and then he would go to Guinevere with a heart from whatever he'd killed.

And he wouldn't have to kill the princess after all.

Twenty-Two

Several days passed before Guinevere had a chance to peer into the magic mirror again, for even with her minimal magic, she recognised an enchantment when she saw one. She hung the looking glass on the wall, on a hook that sat at such a perfect height, it must have been made for it.

She stared at her own reflection for a moment, relieved to see the shadows beneath her eyes had not darkened, even after days of presiding over hearings where Sir Dagonet or Sir Lancelot passed judgement while Melwas glowered at her. That was as close as he'd get to her. She'd barred the door again, and Lancelot stood outside it – unless Melwas could best the knight, which she highly doubted, she would be safe.

"Show me my brother," she whispered to the mirror. The surface misted, before the forest reappeared.

A flickering fire lit the scene, a tableau of butchery if ever she'd seen one. Xylander crouched beside the body of a deer, his arms elbow deep inside the carcass.

"Yes!" he said suddenly, and freed his arms. In one hand, he held a gore-encrusted dagger, and blood streamed from the other, which held…what appeared to be the deer's heart.

Guinevere's stomach churned. She was no stranger to the sight of blood and slaughter, for as castle chatelaine, she'd supervised the killing of the winter's meat stocks for many years now, but something about Xylander's kill reminded her of some ancient, pagan ritual, where the so-called priests sacrificed beasts to their myriad deities. She'd heard tell of some remote places in the deep northern forests where such beliefs were still upheld, but surely such things would have died out by now.

She was willing to bet Princess Zurine would not be watching such slaughter. Guinevere scanned the clearing, but she did not see the princess.

As the girl popped into her head, the image in the mirror blurred, moving too fast to see clearly, as it sped away from Xylander. Too far.

A tiny cottage came into view – not the sort of place a princess belonged, unless she was visiting one of her father's poorer subjects with charity, as Guinevere herself had occasionally done. Maids who had once served in the castle, but were now widows, or new mothers, or that time one of the castle shepherds had broken his leg…

But this cottage was built half into a hillside, hidden beneath some sort of creeping vine, and no smoke came from the chimney, despite the abundance of wood to feed a fire. A deserted place – surely the princess could not be inside!

Guinevere became aware of a rumbling sound. It was a moment before she realised it came not from outside her door but from the mirror.

A cart came into view, pulled by four men. As it slowed to a stop, three more men jumped out, and began to unload the cart. They passed the sacks hand to hand until they reached the cottage door, which the final man shouldered open.

Guinevere held her breath. If the princess truly was inside, this did not bode well for her.

As if on command, the mirror image moved to inside the dimly lit cottage.

One man knelt to light a fire, while the rest moved the sacks to the loft.

"Hey, who drank all the wine? The jug's empty!"

The offending jug sat on the table, next to a single cup.

"The cheese is gone, too."

"Has anyone seen my winter cloak? 'Tis cold in here without the fire roaring."

"Who's that in the bed, then?"

The men crowded around the edge of the pallet on the floor, staring at someone sleeping facedown in the straw.

Even dressed in peasants' clothing, Guinevere recognised the princess.

"He's wearing my new wool tunic!"

"And my spare one!"

"That's my winter cloak!"

"Aren't those the striped stockings you stole off that tinker at the fair?"

"Only because it was dark. What man would wear such womanish stockings?"

Silence swept through them for a moment.

"There's a girl in our bed."

"Who gets to have her first, then?"

A brawl broke out, spilling outside as the tiny cottage could no longer contain the fighting men.

Guinevere's heart stuck in her throat. She wanted to reach through the looking glass and pluck the princess from such peril, but she could do nothing but watch.

One man, bigger than the others, broke away from the fighting to stand in the doorway, looking from the sleeping girl to his still brawling comrades.

"I say we wait," he said.

The fighting stopped.

"Why?"

"We only have a few weeks before snow starts to fall and block the passes back to town. Time enough to mine enough salt to see us through the winter, but only if we don't waste any time with whores."

"I've never seen a whore like that. She must be one of those courty-sans. Rich men's mistresses. With skin white as snow like that…"

"Never mind what she is. She's ours now. Our reward for when winter comes, and whoever mines the most twixt now and then gets her first."

"What'll we do with her 'til then?"

"Women's work. She can cook and clean for us, and when winter comes, she can warm our beds, as well."

"What if she refuses? Courty-sans don't clean stuff. They're like ladies, I heard."

"Then we take her to the local lord to be branded as a thief. Two tunics, a cloak and a jug of wine she's taken so far."

"And the cheese!"

"Men have been hanged for less. She won't

refuse. Not if she wants to live."

"But if she wants to take her chances with the local lord?"

The big man laughed. "Then we don't wait. We each take her, and then take what's left to Lord Melwas. That lord isn't lenient to thieving whores." He gestured to one of the others. "Wake her up. Time to make her an offer."

Guinevere watched in horror as one of the men shook Zurine awake.

The girl let out a shrill scream and backed up against the wall.

The big man made his offer – that they'd let her stay with them, if she did the cooking and cleaning.

Guinevere wanted to scream at the girl to run, to get away while she could, but the terrified princess merely nodded her acceptance.

Guinevere cursed. Where was her brother?

Twenty-Three

When Xylander reached the city, he debated whether to visit an inn to make himself look respectable again before he visited the castle. But without even a change of clothes, he doubted he could do much. Besides, Guinevere would not care what state he was in, as long as he brought good news.

He lingered in the inn long enough to buy a stoppered jug of wine to preserve the heart, before heading up to the castle.

Guinevere sat in the throne room, alone on the dais, while a knight dispensed justice in the

King's name. When his eyes met hers, she beckoned to the knight, who declared the day's audience at an end.

Guinevere headed out of the throne room, and Xylander followed, all the way to the private apartments where she'd stayed before she married the King.

"Where have you been?" she hissed, slamming the door shut behind him.

Xylander bridled. "Why, doing your business, my queen." He sketched a mocking bow, then held out the stoppered wine jug. "As you commanded."

She stared at the jug. "What would I want wine for? What of the princess?"

Xylander uncorked the jug and drew out the dripping heart. The wine sheeting off it almost looked like blood. "Her heart, as promised."

Guinevere's mouth dropped open in horror. "Don't lie to me. I saw you kill that deer. How could you leave the princess in the woods like that?"

Xylander dropped the heart back in the jug. Wine splashed across his tunic, but he ignored it. "How could you know that?"

"Show me the princess!" Guinevere hissed, pointing at a mirror on the wall.

The mirror misted, swirled, then showed an astonishingly clear picture that was not a reflection of the room.

"How…?" he began.

Guinevere hushed him. "Listen and look!"

He peered at the looking glass, and swore. Zurine sat on a rough stool beside a smoky fire, weeping into her hands. When she lifted her head, he saw the dark shadow of a bruise across half her face, as if someone had hit her. "The bread will be better tomorrow. I promise. Please don't hit me again," she whimpered.

Fury rose up. Who had dared strike his princess?

"Why in heaven's name did you leave her with those criminals, and bring me a heart, to make me think she was dead?" Guinevere demanded.

Xylander stared. "You asked for her heart!"

Guinevere stamped her foot. "You fool! I told you to win her heart. You know, make her fall in love with you, so she won't marry Lord Melwas, the King's slimy cousin!"

Win her…? Why hadn't she said so?

"But…"

"You left her in a cottage with criminals! They're stealing salt from one of the King's mines, and selling it…and they mean to take her, too, treating her like a servant for now, but they have a wager…whoever can mine the most salt before the first snowfall will make her his whore!"

Xylander's mouth dropped open, and he couldn't seem to close it. Words failed him.

"Go and find her, you fool, and save her, before it's too late!"

Xylander hurried off, staying in the city only long enough to procure fresh clothes and provisions and a new horse, before he returned to the clearing where he'd last seen Zurine. This time he would follow the hoofprints until he found what he'd missed the first time – signs of where Zurine had gone.

He would not fail her this time.

Twenty-Four

By all that was holy, what had Xylander been thinking? That she wanted the girl dead? If she had, she'd have asked for the princess's head, not her heart. As if she'd ask for anyone's head. What sort of mad queen would demand such a thing?

And that dripping heart...Guinevere shuddered. She might not be squeamish at the sight of blood, but when he'd pulled the organ out of that wine jug, red with wine or blood or a mixture of both...why, she'd challenge even the strongest man not to shrink away at such a sight. It would churn anyone's stomach.

Except Xylander's, of course. They'd called him the Huntsman for a reason back home. When he'd splashed gore down his front from it, he'd barely blinked.

She hoped he hadn't splashed any…Guinevere swore under her breath. There were two distinctive red splatters on her white skirt, and a scatter of droplets on her bodice, too. She would have to change gowns, or appear in court looking like a sloppy serving wench.

Slipping out of her soiled gown was the easy part, but lacing up a new one was harder than she'd expected. She'd never needed a maid when they were laced along the front or the side, but this benighted bloody thing had to be laced up the back…

She dropped the golden gown on the bed, then realised the stain had gone through to her under things. She needed a clean shift, too.

She pulled the fresh linen out of its chest, just as the door slammed open.

"I will see the traitorous whore, and you shall not stand in my way!" Melwas roared as he strode in.

Guinevere clutched her shift to her chest, painfully aware of her nakedness as Melwas' greedy eyes took her in.

"Whore!" Melwas repeated, pointing an accusing finger at her. "I saw your lover leaving. The guards will catch him, and wring a confession out of him, I have no doubt. As for you, you are no more a queen than the lowliest tavern whore. Spreading your legs for every common knight..." From the way his eyes lit up, he looked like he was fairly drooling over the thought.

"Sir Lander is most certainly not my lover!" she said, drawing herself up. She longed to dress, to put layers of wool and linen and maybe even armour between her body and Melwas' leer, but she didn't dare move her shift and expose herself to him. Or Lancelot, who stood behind him with a thunderous expression on his face.

"Take this lying, war-mongering whore to the dungeons!" Melwas ordered.

"Whatever else she may be, she is the Queen, and our sovereign," Lancelot said steadily. "Her guilt is for the King to judge, not you or I."

"Her lover flees the castle, while she stands here, naked as her name day, while the King lies dying in his own chamber! The King will not live to judge her – she'll make sure of that!" Melwas glared. "You saw the answer her father sent. The head of the King's own messenger, with his tongue cut out. King Artorius sent the man a messenger to inform him of their union, but all he received back was a declaration of war! That whore is responsible, I know it!"

Guinevere's heart sank. Her father truly had gone mad, if he cared so little about offending his neighbours that he was willing to execute their messengers.

Lancelot's eyes met hers, cold blue pools that would show her no mercy. "Your Majesty, Lord Melwas accuses you of grave crimes indeed. Until your innocence or guilt can be proven before the King or his duly appointed judge, I must ask you to remain in your chambers, and a guard will stand outside. If I do not do this, the King will never forgive me.

Do you agree to remain in your chambers, my queen?"

"She is a criminal, and she belongs in the dungeons!" Melwas raged.

Lancelot's gaze never wavered. "Your answer, my queen?"

She blew out a breath she'd barely been aware she was holding. "I will stay here. Until…my husband wakes." If by some miracle he woke… Tears formed, threatening to spill, but she held her head high. These men had seen enough. Neither of them would see her cry. "And my condolences for your messenger. If I'd had any idea my father would do such a thing…"

She didn't want to believe it, but in her heart, she did. He truly had gone mad.

Lancelot bowed low. "Thank you, Your Majesty. Now, we will see ourselves out." He seized Melwas' arm and dragged the protesting lord out of the room, kicking the door shut behind him.

Guinevere sagged. She'd panicked so when they burst into her room, she hadn't thought to defend herself. She should have showed them her wine stained gown, explained that Lander was her brother...

The son of a mad king who was now their enemy.

No, she could not tell them about Lander at all, unless he returned with the princess.

She dressed mechanically, and it wasn't until she was done that she realised she'd donned the plainest gown she'd brought from home. The soft, oft-washed linen was comforting, reminding her of happier times. But not comforting enough.

She buried her head in her hands and wept.

For two kingdoms at war, for a beloved father gone mad, for the life of a loyal servant lost, for a loving husband fallen before she could truly know him, for the princess in peril...and perhaps even a tear or two for herself, and the uncertainty her future held.

Twenty-Five

For the third time, Xylander returned to the clearing where he'd lit the fire for Zurine. Rain had erased her horse's tracks, along with any signs of her passage. He hated to admit it, but he'd lost her. How could he save her now?

No matter how much he wanted to…

Not even a hunting dog would help him now, for the same rain that had taken her footprints had surely washed away her scent, too.

He would retrace the path her horse had taken on its own, then return to town, and ask

Guinevere for her magic mirror. If it could show her the princess in some distant cottage, then surely it could show him the path the princess had taken to get there.

He trudged along the muddy trail, wishing she'd left at least something for him to follow. Hadn't there been some ancient princess who'd given a hero a spool of thread to find his way out of a labyrinth?

Wait…was that…a thread?

Not the sort to lead him out of a labyrinth, for it was no longer than his finger, but what drew his attention was that it was white wool – spun wool, which could only have come from someone's clothing. Zurine had been wearing a gown of white wool beneath her black cloak – a snow white maiden, indeed, the fairest he'd ever seen. And he would again, if he could but follow her trail, and find her.

He plucked the thread from the bush that had caught it, and stuck it in his pocket. There was a game trail here, that widened considerably on the other side of the bush. Almost as if someone had hidden it deliberately. The rain had not washed away the signs of deep ruts made from heavily laden carts that had once passed through here.

Guinevere's illegal miners, maybe?

He hastened along the cart track, for that's what it had become, until he happened upon a lady's slipper. Once white, it was now so caked in mud he barely recognised it as Zurine's, but who else but a castle-bred princess would wear such a shoe out here?

Five hundred yards further, he found the second shoe, half hidden under a thorn bush that held no less than three white threads, including one as long as his arm.

She had passed this way, for certain. All he had to do was find her, and save her.

A fitting quest for a noble knight. Maybe even a prince.

Twenty-Six

"I must interrogate the prisoner!"

Every night Melwas appeared at the door of her chamber, and each night he uttered the same demand. But the guards would not allow him to enter, to Guinevere's endless relief.

Until tonight.

"Yes, Lord Regent, but you say she is a witch who has cast a spell over the King. What if she were to do the same to you?"

"I am immune to magic! I have a charm that wards me against evil such as hers!"

"Let me see that." There was a long pause,

followed by, "You should send your guards to arrest whoever sold that to you, Lord Regent, for it is about as magical as my left arse-cheek."

"Later, later. What matters is this traitor, and I must interrogate her now!"

"Very well, Lord Regent."

As the door swung open, Guinevere rose to stand before the mirror, hiding it from sight. She couldn't bear to see poor Zurine enslaved to those monsters, so she rarely looked at it, except to follow her brother's search, but she did not want Melwas to notice it and take it from her. Or Lancelot, who claimed to be able to sense magic.

She met his expressionless eyes as he stood behind Melwas. Melwas made to shut the door, but he could not with Lancelot in the way.

"Move, man, I must speak to her alone!" Melwas insisted, rubbing his groin as he turned fever-bright eyes on Guinevere.

"For your own protection, I cannot allow that," Lancelot said, folding his arms across his chest.

"This girl is no danger to me." Melwas strode toward Guinevere.

She backed away from him, until her shoulders touched cold stone and could go no further. Still he advanced.

She turned her face away.

His hand closed around her throat.

"You see, Lancelot? She knows who's in charge here."

"King Artorius, my husband," she choked out.

Melwas' hand squeezed, cutting off her air. "What did you do to him, witch? Undo the spell you cast on our beloved king, and perhaps I will let you live."

"I did nothing…nothing!" she said.

He slammed her head against the wall so hard her vision exploded into stars for a moment. "Lying whore!" Then he slapped her face.

Guinevere tasted blood. The magic within her roared to be released, to defend her, but she forced it down. If she cast a spell, they would know her to be a witch, and she would seal her fate for sure.

"I swear on my life, I did nothing to hurt the King," she managed to say.

"Faithless Flamish bitch!" Melwas shoved his body against hers, pinning her to the wall. "Tell the truth and I will let you live. Continue to lie…and you'll wish you had taken my offer." He ground his hips against her, the hardness between them pressing against her belly.

Bile rose up in her throat.

"I never…" she began, but he slapped her a second time, so hard her head rang. Her lip stung, as if she'd cut it.

He grinned at her, running a finger over her lip. It came away bloody. "You'll bleed far more for me, bitch. Just like the queen before you. So much you'll beg to die, just like she did." He sucked his bloodied finger.

Then his eyes rolled up in his head and he keeled over, snoring.

Guinevere's eyes met Lancelot's knowing ones. He knew she'd cast a sleeping spell.

"Guards!" he shouted.

She shrank away to the corner furthest from the door and the downed Melwas. Wishing she could disappear entirely.

The guards arrived, panting and wide-eyed as they took in the sight of their quailing queen and the regent in repose.

"Pick up the Lord Regent and carry him to his bedchamber," Lancelot instructed. "No man is to enter the Queen's chamber alone."

The men did as they were bidden, shooting frightened glances at Guinevere.

When Lancelot alone stood in the doorway, she dared to step out of the shadows. Smoothing her skirts to disguise how much her hands shook, she lifted her eyes to meet his. Her husband's most loyal, honourable knight knew her secret now. She had nothing left to hide.

He regarded her for a long moment. Almost as if he was daring her to bespell him as she had Melwas.

Magic had been forced out of her once, but she had better control over it now. "If I had the power to heal him, I would," she said softly. "King Artorius, I mean." Not Melwas.

Sir Lancelot inclined his head. "I will send your maids with hot water so that you might bathe. I will stand guard over your chamber tonight. Sleep well." And he left, closing the door behind him.

A bath. How had he known she'd want to wash off Melwas' touch? Surely the man could not read minds. Few men could use magic, and she hadn't sensed any in him.

Not even in his left arse-cheek, as he'd so coarsely put it.

She smothered a laugh. Now she'd be thinking about the knight's backside, instead of worrying about what he'd do now he knew she was a witch.

Twenty-Seven

He found Zurine's camp by mid-afternoon. There was evidence of a fire – she'd watched him more carefully than he'd realised, that night they'd spent in the woods together – and he found the wax rind of the cheese they'd shared.

He could keep going, or make camp, as she had.

If he knew she was close by, that he'd reach her by nightfall, he would have continued on without hesitation. But he didn't know how long she'd wandered until she'd found the cottage, or the cottage inhabitants had found her. She could still be days away, and he'd be no use to her if he arrived without having slept. Fighting one man he might manage…but seven of them? Hardened miners might not be fighters, but they knew where to strike a blow and how to make it a good one. A man who could split rock could split bone and flesh with ease.

Seven of them…he would need a plan.

Because he would save Zurine, or die trying. And he did not intend to die.

No, he had too much living to do.

Twenty-Eight

Guinevere's days blended into a monotony where she had little to do other than stare at the mirror. She only knew a new day had dawned when the guard outside her door changed colour, for the knights wore their bright surcoats while on guard duty as well as at court. Warned by Lancelot not to speak to her, lest she try to bespell them as well, none of the knights would meet her eyes or offer their names, so she named them for their blazons.

The knight with a lying-down lion was

Sleepy, while the knight who bore a serpent twisted about a staff was the Physician. A different guard for each day of the week, until Lancelot returned to stand guard. Though she knew his name, she found herself thinking of him as Grumpy. Not for the fine sword embroidered on his breast, but for the thunderous expression on his face whenever he saw her.

Whatever approval he'd had for her at first, it had faded fast, replaced by his barely concealed anger as he watched the maidservants bring her food or clean her chamber.

"I am not responsible for the King's illness," she declared to him one morning.

He raised surprised eyes to meet hers for a moment, before looking away again.

Nettled, she added, "Nor am I unfaithful."

He winced, though he did not meet her eyes again.

She stamped her foot. "Look at me, damn you! Look in my eyes and see I'm telling the truth. You must believe me. I have done nothing to harm your king!"

Lancelot sighed and raised his head. "It matters not what I believe, Your Majesty. It is the King's judgement that matters, and until he is well enough to hold court, or the crown passes to another, I will do as I have always done. I will serve my king and his kingdom."

He hadn't spoken to her since. Not that it mattered.

Xylander journeyed through the forest, day after day, but he had not yet reached the princess. The castle grew colder, and she knew the first winter snows were not far off. She could only pray that her brother reached the princess first.

Twenty-Nine

"What happened to the queen before me?" Guinevere asked her maids one morning. Melwas' words had returned to her, plaguing her sleep, so that she could not rest until she vowed to seek an answer. "How did she die?"

The two girls looked at one another. "Do you mean Queen Viviana, Princess Zurine's mother?"

Guinevere reined in her impatience. The maids were not at fault for her own ignorance. "If she was the last queen, then yes."

"Everyone thought she loved the King as

much as he loved her, but one night when the King was away, she was discovered abed with one of Lord Melwas' sworn knights. Lord Melwas himself caught them, and in shame, the queen took her own life. She buried a dagger in her breast. 'Twas said she could not face her husband, so she killed herself before the King returned."

Guinevere shuddered. What a horrible end. "What of the knight?"

"Executed for treason at Lord Melwas' command."

That surprised her. Surely Melwas would have rejoiced that his man had successfully seduced and dishonoured the queen. She didn't doubt how happy he'd be if it had happened to her.

"My mother said she saw Lord Melwas entering the queen's chambers, the first night the King was away. She heard the queen cry out, but he'd barred the door, so she could not get in. The next morning, the queen would not let anyone bathe her, but Mother saw the bruises when she helped her dress. She said it went on for weeks. Fresh bruises, every morning, until the day the queen died."

The other girl hushed her. "He's Lord Regent now. You can't go accusing him of such things!"

"You don't know what goes on here of a night, for you sleep in town and not the castle. Since the King's been ill, no woman in the castle is safe, unless she's in the kitchen, for there's always someone about there. I've taken to sleeping in the corner by the pantry, myself. Did you see Helga this morning? She could scarcely walk. Melwas is a mean one, and no mistake."

What was wrong with men? First her father, now Melwas and his late knight, not to mention the miners who had Zurine. They were little more than animals, rutting like it was their right to own women's bodies as well as their own. If a woman dared to take her pleasure of a man without his consent, there would be uproar, but if a man did it…whispered rumours and a warning to stay silent was all that happened.

Guinevere wished her magic was stronger, capable of more than just a sleeping spell.

She'd settle for turning Melwas' manhood into a venomous snake that bit him and made him swell up purple and green until he died screaming.

She hoped when Xylander found the men who had Zurine, he killed them all.

While she watched.

She dismissed her maids, and settled down to watch the mirror while she broke her fast. Xylander had to be close now, and she didn't want to miss a moment.

Thirty

Xylander passed the spot three times where the track ended before he'd thought to push at what appeared to be an impenetrable hedge. Lo and behold, it was in fact a thin screen of branches fastened to a sackcloth frame that swung open at a touch.

The cottage and the mine beyond were exactly as they had appeared in Guinevere's mirror, which meant the bruises he'd seen on Zurine's face had not been a lie.

How dare any man strike her – the heir to the throne, no less! As if stealing salt were not treason enough. When Zurine was safely home in her castle, he would lead a troop of guards back here to deal justice in its most brutal form.

He dismounted, leading his horse into a hidden dell on the other side of the screen, out of sight of both the cottage and the mine. He was a hunter, not some sort of berserker knight – his talents lay in stealth and cunning, not pitched battle against seven burly men. Though if it came to it…he would have no qualms about drawing his sword and dispensing justice early. But that would upset Zurine, so it was best to keep violence to a last resort, at least while she was watching. Later, the blood would flow.

He crept back to the cottage, circling around it to see if there was any movement. No one was in sight, and the men kept no livestock – not even a goat for milk.

Xylander watched for a while longer, before he decided the men could only be in either the house or the mine. A thin wisp of smoke curled up from the cottage chimney, and the scent of something savoury reached him. Stew of some sort, he suspected. Someone was home.

He chose a spot out of sight of the door and pressed his ear to the wooden wall. Not a sound reached his ears. Either they were all too busy eating, or the cook was the only person home. He listened longer, but there was no change. The cottage was as quiet as the grave.

Uttering a quick prayer that he would find Zurine inside, he drew his sword. Holding the blade down by his side, hidden in the folds of his cloak, he pushed open the door. He put his back to the solid oak boards, and kept pushing until it hit the wall. No one hiding behind the door, waiting to ambush him, then, but it took a moment for his eyes adjust to the dim interior.

Movement, then a faint cry as someone stumbled, made him bring his blade up in readiness.

"Please, don't hurt me!" came Zurine's plaintive cry.

Xylander's heart constricted in his chest. No lady, let alone a princess, should have to utter such words with a knight in the room.

"Are you alone?" he demanded.

She nodded. "They are all at work." Then a peculiar expression came over her face. "But they will come for their noon meal, as soon as I ring the bell." She pointed her spoon at a rusted cauldron that hung from the ceiling. Her unspoken words hung in the air – she could call aid in a moment.

His heart twisted. She might fear the miners, but she did not trust him, either.

He closed the door behind him and sheathed his sword, holding his hands up in surrender. "I have come to rescue you from these terrible men, Princess. Come, and I shall take you home." He held out his hand.

"You!" she hissed, wide-eyed, as she scrambled away from him, deeper into the cottage. "You're her assassin! The knight she sent to kill me, not rescue me!"

His heart sank. "Princess, I swear to you, I mean you no harm."

She crossed the patch of uneven straw that must serve as the communal bed, putting her back to the wall before she slowly rose to her feet. "How do you know who I am, then?

None of them know. No one would recognise me like this!" She waved her hand at her peasant clothing. She wore a roughspun tunic, the muddy brown colour helping her blend into the cottage wall, that ended halfway to her knees. Her white skirt hung in brown tatters beneath, as if she'd fought an army of thorn bushes.

Or a pack of men, intent on stealing her virtue.

He forced that thought away. He had to win her trust before he could ask anything else.

"I would recognise you anywhere, Your Highness," he admitted. "I first saw you in the tourney your father held for your name-day. Your beauty bewitched me so that I could think of nothing else – least of all the lance coming toward me."

She stared at him for a moment, before her eyes widened. "Are you...the Green Knight?"

He bowed his head. "To my endless shame, yes. My dented helmet stuck to my head, but even if it hadn't, my eyes were too full of the sight of you to see anything else that day. By the time I'd had help wrenching the helmet off, you were nowhere to be seen, and I had lost the tourney, so I dared not face you. I returned to Castrum recently, only to hear you were missing. I thought, perhaps, I might redeem myself in your eyes if I could rescue you from your captors. And here you are. Now, we must flee, before those wretched men return."

Zurine's eyes took on a haunted, hollow cast. "I cannot come with you. They told me if I tried to leave, they would hunt me down, and drag me before Melwas, the lord of these lands, as a thief. And they will beat me."

As they had already, and would again, if she remained, her eyes seemed to lament, though her lips fell silent.

"But Lord Melwas is your cousin. Surely he would help you," Xylander began.

She shook her head. "Melwas would likely not recognise me like this. I barely recognise me, and if they bruise my face any more...my own father would not know me. And if by some miracle Melwas did manage to identify me, he would force me into a marriage I do not want. He would lock me in his dungeons until I agreed to do his bidding, just like he did to my mother. It will be the death of me, for I would welcome the kiss of a blade far more readily than my cousin's touch. I am safer here."

"With the common men in this cottage? Men who beat you and treat you like a servant? Who share your bed…" Fury choked him up too much to continue.

Her eyes blazed. "They are as chivalrous as any knight. There is but one bed, yes, but none of them has dared lay a hand upon me, and should one man even suggest it, his fellows beat the idea out of his head. They only beat me if I fail to cook a meal to their liking, which is my fault. I deserved this," she said, waving at her face. "I lied, saying I knew how to cook. But if I told them the truth, they would take me to Melwas, or…to her…"

Xylander shook his head. Poor, innocent princess – she had no idea of the wager the men had made. A wager she would pay the price for, if she stayed here. And if she left…he had to make sure the men could not follow her.

He took a deep breath. "If I swear, on my life and all I hold dear, that I will keep you safe and take you from here to wherever you wish to go, and no one, be they a lord or an assassin or anyone, will touch you again without your consent, let alone beat you or throw you in a dungeon…would you trust me enough to come with me?"

She bit her lip. There was longing in her eyes – longing to believe him, he hoped – but she shook her head. "You can't protect me from all of them. There are seven big, strong men, and they will follow us."

He caught her hands in his. "I have a swift horse, and I know the woods as well as any hunter. They may try to follow, but they will not find us. I swear to you, Princess."

Tears filled her eyes as she opened her mouth to refuse again.

He touched a finger to her lips. "I will return on the morrow, and I will save you. Until then, rest, for we will have a long journey ahead of us."

She shrugged off his touch. "How can I sleep, knowing that on the morrow, I will meet my doom? At your hands or theirs or Melwas…what does it matter?"

"Things will turn out well. This I swear to you," Xylander said desperately, though he did not yet know how. Somehow, between now and the morrow, he had to kill seven men and survive to save the princess. He needed a plan…and probably a miracle, too. Or magic. Which gave him an idea. "Do you still have my magic apple?" The one she'd stolen from him in the woods, after one bite had sent him to sleep.

Her eyes narrowed for a moment, before she thrust her hand into her pocket and pulled out the apple. It looked like he'd taken a bite from it barely a moment before, not days ago. A magic apple, indeed. "I thought it was poisoned, when you fell over dead," she said.

The thought of Guinevere poisoning anyone – let alone him! – made Xylander laugh. "It was a gift from my sister to help me sleep, no more. A bite from that apple grants me the sweetest night's sleep I have ever known. Here, lie down, take a bite, and see."

She lifted up the apple, squinting at it.

"After the men have eaten their noon meal. It is almost ready, and they will be angry with me if I burn it, or call them too late." A shudder shook her shoulders.

Resolve hardened within Xylander. These bastards who'd dared to beat his princess would not live past the morrow. He would kill them all himself. Only then would she be safe.

"Then I will return on the morrow, Princess. Until then, I pray that your dreams will be sweet." Xylander bowed and left.

It sat ill with him to leave her with the men another night, but the clear skies promised it would not snow today or tomorrow, so she should be safe. All he needed was a plan – a plan to kill seven men, armed with picks and axes and shovels, while all he carried was a single sword.

There had to be a way to complete his quest. And if he stayed awake all night, he would find it, and enact it.

For with Zurine's life at stake, he could not live with himself if he did any less.

Thirty-One

"No, you fool, go back in there and carry her out! You would not leave me in such danger! She's barely half your size – even if she fights you, you must!" Guinevere hissed at the image of her brother in the mirror, but neither Zurine or Xylander heard her.

Just as long as the guard outside the door did not hear her, either. The last time the Physician knight had heard her talking to herself, he'd summoned Lancelot, convinced she'd managed to sneak someone into her chamber to conspire with.

Lancelot had duly searched her chamber, while his colleague kept watch from the doorway. She'd stood with her arms folded across her breast, not having to feign her disdain for their baseless suspicions. After peering under all the furniture, Lancelot had declared himself satisfied, and turned to leave.

"But what about in the chests? You could hide a man or even two in one of those!" the Physician had insisted.

Dutifully, Lancelot had gone through her gowns, laying them one by one on the bed until an armload of fabric slithered out of the folds of the golden gown.

Guinevere's cheeks had grown hot as Lancelot lifted up a silk shift, so gossamer thin she could see straight through it. The King had gifted her with half a dozen such scandalous shifts, and the one time she'd dared to try wearing one, the sensuous slide of silk over her skin had made her think of a lover's hands, of...doing things a maiden should not be considering. So she'd stuffed them inside the gold silk skirt, too embarrassed to look at them again.

Lancelot's eyes had seemed to burn into her very soul at that moment, as if he could read her thoughts. She'd ducked her head, but it was too late.

"The Queen is clearly not hiding anyone in her undergarments," she'd heard him say, before he returned her things to their proper place and shut the lid. "Leave the Queen to her solitude, Tristan, for she is surely praying for the King's recovery."

The moment he'd left, she'd pressed her burning cheeks against the stone walls to cool them, but she hadn't been able to shake the thought of a lover's hands stroking her through silk. Especially if those strong hands belonged to Sir Lancelot...

But now, she shook the memory from her mind. Xylander had climbed a tree, from which he could observe the cottage and its inhabitants, and Zurine remained inside.

Guinevere didn't trust the girl. There was something wild in the way she'd spoken to Xylander, more like a spooked horse than a damsel whose distress would soon be at an end.

Zurine heard a sound – the voices of the men leaving the mine, no doubt – and her frightened expression turned to one of firm resolve.

"If I cannot have my prince, then none shall have me," Zurine said.

She lifted the apple to her lips, and took a bite. Then another.

Her eyelids drooped, but determination drove her. She wolfed down the apple, even as she swayed, falling to her knees on the straw pallet, until finally, nothing but the core remained. It rolled out of her hand as she subsided on the straw, falling into an enchanted sleep so deep, her chest barely rose with each shallow breath.

A slumber so complete, one might think the princess was dead.

Thirty-Two

If he could collapse the mine entrance, or somehow block it, he might be able to take them all out at once, Xylander mused. But without a siege weapon like a trebuchet, which would take far more than a day to build, there was no way he'd be able to accomplish such a feat without a small army.

He could possibly fell one of the bigger oak trees, which, if it fell just right, would block the entrance, though he doubted it would be heavy enough to collapse it. If he were to venture inside the mine to inspect it, while the men were asleep, perhaps, he might find a way to sabotage one of the tunnels, or the entrance itself, but he would have to be close to spring the trap. Close enough to possibly get caught in the cave-in, and what would happen to Zurine then?

He had a crossbow in his saddlebag. It was not the most honourable of weapons, but he'd used it against a boar or two when one of his companions' spears had broken. Saved the man's life, too. But there was little honour in slaughtering this kind of common filth, so what did it matter if he shot them with a crossbow? The very oak he'd considered felling to block the mine entrance would make a good vantage point from which to target the men as they came out. In less than a minute, he could despatch all seven, if his aim was true and he did not miss. And if they did not realise where he was shooting from and take shelter.

What if…

Voices drew his attention to the mine entrance. Four men had already emerged, shouldering their mining tools as they headed back to the house.

But Zurine had not rung the bell to summon them to dinner – why had they come out early? Did they know he was here? Xylander retreated deeper into the foliage, praying they would not see him. If he lost the element of surprise, then it was still just one man against seven, and Zurine would be the loser.

Something he could not allow to happen.

Seven men moved in single file to the cottage, propping their tools up against the wall before they went in.

If Zurine were not inside, he might set fire to the place, trapping them inside...

Xylander dismissed that idea as quickly as it had come. Too dangerous, for Zurine was surely asleep inside, and he did not dare risk her.

"Why is our dinner not ready?" one of the men roared. "Do you need reminding of your duties?" He raised his fist, striding inside.

"The slattern's asleep!" someone else said.

"Then get her up! Who does she think she is, lying abed when there is work to be done?"

Someone sniggered. "The Queen, maybe.

All the Queen does is lie on her back for the King."

"She won't wake!" This voice sounded panicked. "She's not breathing!"

"She can't be dead. We have a wager."

"Someone came into our house and slew her while we worked? When I find the man, I'll bury my pick in his belly, I will!"

"There's no blood or blade. Naught but this apple core." The offending core flew out of the door.

Xylander's heart stopped. One bite of the apple would have sent her to sleep. To eat the whole thing…she might sleep for weeks, or never wake at all. Unless someone broke the spell.

Guinevere had told him how once, but he was damned if he could remember. All he knew was that it didn't need a witch to break the spell.

"What'll we do?" a man wailed.

"We'll put her in the meat chest, so she'll stay fresh. First snowfall can't be that far off – a few days, maybe. When it comes, we'll pull her out and have her then. She'll last longer if she don't fight back. We might each get two or three turns at her."

They thought she was dead, yet they intended to violate her corpse? These men were worse than animals.

Xylander clenched his fists as he watched one man carry her limp body from the cottage to the mine.

"Will she fit?" worried a man who trotted close on the first man's heels.

"Of course she will," said another, striding behind. "We had two boars in there last summer, remember? The meat stayed fresh for months."

They intended to place her in a chest where they'd kept pigs?

Xylander's rage simmered, close to boiling.

"We could keep her in there for months, take her out at night for a poke, then put her back. Like having a whore you don't need to pay."

No one called Zurine a whore.

The seventh man disappeared inside the mine as Xylander slid down the tree. The moment his feet touched the ground, he drew his sword.

He glanced at the mining tools, discarded by the door.

Seven unarmed pigs, waiting to be slaughtered.

He didn't have long to wait.

The first man emerged, hauling himself out of the hole and onto the turf. He never even saw the sword that pierced his throat. He was dead before he could make a sound.

Xylander kicked the corpse aside.

The second man was the one who'd called her a whore.

Blinded by rage, Xylander lost all control.

Some time later – he did not know how long – he paused to catch his breath. Had he gotten them all?

He glanced around. He counted six…no, seven heads, for the last had rolled down the slope after he lopped it off. The turf was now more red than green, so he wiped his blade on a dead man's tunic before sheathing it.

Some of them must have fought back, he realised, tasting blood as he massaged his aching jaw. But it hadn't been enough to save them. Nothing would.

Now, nothing stood between him and Zurine. He would save her, just as he'd promised.

Xylander slid down the ladder, into the darkness.

Thirty-Three

Xylander followed the light of a flickering candle to the chamber where Zurine lay. The walls glittered, throwing back reflections like pools of water, if ever water pooled vertically. Salt crunched underfoot, but he paid it no heed. Zurine was all that mattered, and she could not be dead.

When he entered her chamber, he gasped. What those dullards had called their meat chest was in fact an enormous casket, carved out of salt so clear he could see her inside it. Zurine lay sleeping beneath an equally transparent lid that was little more than a giant slab of salt.

Xylander levered it aside, and reached inside to pull her out. He touched her bruised throat, and almost cried when he felt her faint pulse. She lived, and once he worked out how to wake her...

A few drops of cold water on her neck did not rouse her, nor did calling her name.

He wished Guinevere were here – it was her blood that had cast the spell, so she would certainly know how to undo it.

Blood? Was that the answer?

He touched his still bleeding lip – split by a lucky punch before he'd hacked the man's hand from his arm – and his fingers came away red.

Lightly, he brushed his bloodstained fingers against her throat, and waited

But she did not wake.

By all that was holy, how had one of his hunting party broken the spell before? He'd drunk too much wine and taken a bite of one of Guinevere's apples to stave off the hangover, but one of his men had stumbled over him in the dark, kicking him in the face.

He'd awoken with the taste of blood in his mouth, and a curse on his lips for every clumsy, drunken fool who'd ever...

Was that it? She had to taste blood to wake?

No. Xylander shied away from even the thought of raising a hand against her. He was not like the men who had kept her captive. He'd come to save her, not hurt her further.

But...perhaps a drop of his blood...

Guinevere had told tales of princesses awoken by a kiss, but he had not believed them. Yet...

He leaned over, and lightly touched his lips to hers.

For a moment, she stiffened, and then her lips parted. To kiss him back!

For the second time that afternoon, Xylander lost control. Her kiss blinded him, drenching his senses until he could see and feel nothing but her. Could not taste the blood, but a faint trace of...apple...

She shoved him away.

"How dare you, assassin!"

Somehow, she'd managed to get her hands on his dagger, which she now pointed at him.

Xylander backed away.

"I mean you no harm, Princess, I swear." He swallowed. "I only kissed you to break the spell, to save you."

"I will not die dishonoured. Not at your hands, or theirs. I will not share my mother's fate," she said, turning the dagger until it pointed at her own breast.

"No!" He dived forward, wresting the weapon from her before she could plunge it into her flesh. "I am not an assassin, I told you!"

"Then who are you?" she demanded.

He could resist her no longer. He'd tried, and failed. "I am Prince Xylander, come to claim you as my bride. But when you disappeared, I set out to find you. That first night, I had hoped to persuade you to return with me, but you ran from me. I searched and searched, until I found you here. I vowed to bring you safely home to Castrum, for that is where you belong. At my side, if you'll have me."

Her eyes widened. "You're the prince my father promised?"

Xylander bowed his head. "Your father sent a messenger to my father, summoning me to Castrum to claim you. Since the day of the tourney, I have thought of no one else. Yet when I saw you in the Great Hall, you stole my breath away with your beauty. I am, and have always been, your prince." He bowed low before her.

She rose unsteadily to her feet, and Xylander moved to help her.

"You're really...real?" she asked, wondering eyes shimmering with tears.

"Yes, Your Highness."

"You saved me!" She threw herself at his chest and burst into tears.

Thirty-Four

People rushed through the corridors of the castle, their voices raised in panic. Something was happening, but no one had dared open the door to tell Guinevere what. She would have to ask the maid who brought her noon meal, she decided.

Unless Xylander had returned with the princess…

Guinevere hurried to the mirror, which she'd ignored for some days now. Knowing Xylander had succeeded in winning Zurine's heart and each day brought them closer to

Castrum, she hadn't felt the need to check on their progress.

That, and the couple spent an ordinate amount of time kissing.

Fortunately, she seemed to have caught them at a moment their tongues weren't tangled together, as they rode through the forest.

"We'll reach the road soon, Princess. When we do, it's less than a day's ride to Castrum – I'll have you in your own bed by nightfall," Xylander said.

Zurine giggled. "And I thought you wanted to wait until after we were wed. What if I plan to have you in your bed tonight, instead, my prince?"

Guinevere hurriedly told the mirror to show her reflection before the conversation turned any more intimate. She didn't want to know what her brother and his (hopefully) soon to be wife wanted to do to each other in bed.

But if they were still a day away, then the castle commotion could not be because of their arrival.

Hope sparked in her breast. Maybe a

miracle had occurred, and the King had recovered!

Obedient to her mind's desire, the mirror showed an image of Artorius, lying unmoving in his bed. People moved around the periphery, blocking her vision, until a voice she recognised at Lancelot's said roughly, "Move aside! The physician is here!"

A true physician, and not the knight she called by that name, shuffled forward, and the crowd parted.

Guinevere's heart sank, feeling for all the world like it had turned to stone within her chest and dropped into a bottomless well. The grey-faced corpse in the King's bed had taken all hope from her when he drew his last breath.

Regret washed over her. She, as his wife, should have held his hand in his final moments, waking him from the sleeping spell to let him say a final farewell, if he'd been capable of such a thing. If he'd died alone…

She stared at the mirror. "Can you show me how he died?" she asked.

The image blurred, then cleared. The same man in the same bed, but now Artorius only appeared to be sleeping, his face a pink picture of health on one side, still drooping on the other.

"Your time is over, old man," said a voice Guinevere also recognised. Melwas.

She watched in horror as Melwas took one of the King's pillows, and placed it over his face. He held it down for what seemed an eternity, before he finally took it away again. Artorius, still enchanted by her sleeping spell, had not even fought for his last breath, nor had he been aware of it. That living, sleeping face had turned as grey as the shadow that now lay over the kingdom.

A kingdom ruled by the King's killer.

She wasn't sure what was worse in a king – her father's madness, or Melwas's mad quest for power. She wished she had played more at politics, in her father's court as well as here. Perhaps then she would know how to cheat Melwas out of his stolen crown. Instead, her mother had trained her in how to hold a funeral or coronation feast – neither of which she would be allowed to plan, with Lady Ragna ruling the castle.

When Xylander returned, she would tell him of Melwas' crimes, and he could bring the man to justice. As dowager queen, any power she might have had as Artorius' wife would now pass to Zurine. She would surely help Xylander, for she was certainly no friend of Melwas'.

She sat on the end of her bed, wishing she could do more than wait. But there was no work to be done – her hands sat idle.

The door burst open, and Melwas stood there, his eyes bulging in his red face as if the King had tried to suffocate him and not the other way around .

"There's the traitorous witch! Seize her!"

Guards spilled into the room, grabbing her arms and crowding around her so she could not escape, even if she'd had a mind to, or anywhere else to go.

"Can you hear them?" Melwas asked.

The scurrying servants? Of course she'd heard them…but as Guinevere listened, she realised the sounds outside had grown louder. No longer individual shouts, from outside there came a swelling roar.

"They're baying for your blood, witch. They want justice for their murdered king," Melwas hissed.

Even her patience had its limits. She would not let him get away with this. "You – " she began.

Something struck the back of her head, and blackness won.

Thirty-Five

The roaring in Guinevere's ears only made her head pound all the more. Her arms hurt, too, and she could scarcely feel her hands. She'd expected cold, metal manacles, but instead rough rope wrapped around her wrists, dragging her arms high above her head so that her slippered toes only just touched the stone floor.

She wanted to shout to Melwas that he would regret this, but the gag in her mouth turned her words into a garbled mess.

Someone grabbed her hair, pulling hard.

"Here she is! The traitor who seduced and killed your king. What would you have me do with her?"

"Burn her!"

"Hang her!"

"Flay the flesh from her bones!"

"Put out her eyes!"

"Cut off her head!"

"A week in the stocks, naked!"

"Burn the bitch!"

She could not shut out the voices, for there were too many of them.

But Guinevere had never been a coward. She would meet the eyes of her accusers, even if she could not speak in her defence.

Something scratchy tickled her ankles. Straw, forked onto the stone platform beneath her feet by two burly farmers whose cries of, "Burn her!" seemed to light an unholy fire in their eyes.

The straw piled up beneath her, until her heels sank into it, taking some of her weight from her aching arms.

She'd expected a dungeon, but Melwas had taken her instead to the public square, and tied her to the whipping post where common criminals received their punishment. The stocks stood empty before her. Melwas had not wanted anyone else distracting the mob.

"Traitors to the crown must die. Hanging's too good for her. I say she should burn, like the devil she worships!" Melwas shouted.

Cries of assent drowned out the suggestions for other punishments they wanted her to endure first.

Melwas met her eyes, and Guinevere did her best to glare back. As soon as Xylander arrived, he would save her. She knew it.

"You could have warmed my bed, like Viviana did before you. But you're as stupid and stubborn as Zurine, like all women, which is why men are born to rule. Smart women are obedient, lying on their backs and taking what they're given. Even the women in the crowd know that." Melwas swept a hand around, encompassing the screaming mob. "They want the King's killer, and I'm giving them you."

She tried to bite through the gag, to scream that she knew he was the King's killer, not her, but she did not have the strength.

A gap opened up in the crowd to let a cart through. Men climbed atop it to take the wood, throwing it at her feet, piling it around the little stone platform until she stood on a pyre.

"Lord Regent! The princess has returned!"

The crowd fell silent, faggots falling from suddenly hesitant hands.

Melwas looked around, his panic showing for just a moment, before he shouted, "Keep piling it up! I will go tell the princess we have caught the traitor, and when we return, together we shall watch her burn!"

A ragged cheer rose up, and the pyre began to pile higher.

If the princess heard, then so would Xylander, and he would come to save her. He had to. As long as he was in time…

Silently, Guinevere prayed for a miracle.

Thirty-Six

Zurine dozed against Xylander's back, half hidden beneath his cloak. The soft warmth of her brought a smile to his lips that would not leave his face. Not even when he answered the guards' challenge as he approached the city gates.

"I have brought Princess Zurine safe home!" he announced, when the guard seemed unlikely to open the gates for him.

Gasps went up, and Zurine stirred.

"You are home, Princess," he murmured.

"What's happening over in the square?" she

asked sleepily.

Xylander turned to survey the crowd. "Someone is tied to the whipping post. An execution, or punishment of some sort. Blood always does get the common people excited."

Zurine shuddered. Her arms tightened around him. "Please, I don't want to see. Take me home."

"As my princess commands," he said, turning his horse away.

"We will send word to Lord Regent Melwas that the princess has returned," one of the guards said.

"Tell whoever you please, but she needs rest, and will see no one before the morrow," Xylander said.

"Lord Melwas will want – "

"I don't care what Melwas wants. He is not the king here," Xylander snapped.

The guard's eyes widened. "But the King is dead, and Lord Melwas is Regent until…"

"Until Princess Zurine is crowned queen. Then send word to the castle to prepare for her coronation."

"My father is dead?" Zurine buried her face

in his shoulder and wept. "Oh, Xylander…"

The guard squinted at him. "And who are you, to be giving orders?"

This was the moment he had hoped never to happen, but for Zurine he would do it. "I am Prince Xylander, Princess Zurine's betrothed, and your future king."

Thirty-Seven

The wood had piled so high, Guinevere could no longer see the crowd, though she could hear them. Still Xylander did not come.

Doubt began to creep in. A proper princess would have been rescued by now, but no matter how much she'd loved her mother's tales, she'd never expected to be in one.

If today was her day to die...then she would do so with dignity. No tears, for queens did not cry where her people could see. She prayed her brother would forgive her for saddling him with the throne he had not wanted, and that he would forgive himself when he arrived too late.

Perhaps…no one could have saved her.

She felt a kinship with Queen Viviana, who had at least been able to choose the time and method of her death, but Melwas had not made the mistake of leaving Guinevere with a blade. Then, she might have been able to cut her hands free, and take the only escape open to her, for Guinevere could not escape the mob milling around the square.

A shadow fell on her. Someone standing atop the stacked wood. She stared steadily at the branch before her, refusing to meet the eyes of a man who believed Melwas' lies.

Something flashed overhead. The rope holding her wrists fell away, and her arms dropped heavily to her sides, twin dead weights, as her hands began to tingle painfully with returning circulation.

A hand appeared before her face. "Take it, my queen."

Not Xylander.

She tried to clasp his hand, but her stiff fingers would not do her bidding. After a long moment, he reached down and seized her around the waist instead, drawing her up beside him.

"She is still your queen!" Lancelot thundered. "How dare you judge her? The King is barely cold in his bed, and this is how you treat his beloved queen?"

The shouts that had been so sure before, sounded uncertain now in the face of Lancelot's cold fury.

"The new queen will be crowned, and she will stand in judgement. Until then, anyone who so much as whispers a word against Queen Guinevere will answer to me!" Lancelot lifted Guinevere into his arms, as effortlessly as she suspected he'd done for many a damsel. "Go home, good people of Castrum. Go home and mourn your king!"

The crowd parted for him, leaving him a clear path to the castle.

A princess would have swooned, but Guinevere clung stubbornly to consciousness, concentrating on freeing herself from her gag. When the crowd was far enough behind them not to hear her, she said, "I can walk, you know."

"Better that they see your weakness, my queen. Save your strength," Lancelot said.

For the trial ahead. It should be Melwas on trial, not her. "I didn't kill the King!" she snapped. "Melwas did. Suffocated him in his sleep. With a cushion."

Lancelot's tone did not change. Calm and steady, like she wished her heartbeat was right now. "And how do you know this, my queen? Did you see him do it?"

"In a fashion," she said. Ah, what did she have left to lose? Only her life, and she owed that to him anyway. "I will show you. And the princess."

"You will show me. I will decide what to show the princess."

Slowly, Guinevere nodded. That seemed fair.

"There is a mirror on the wall of my chamber. A magic mirror. Bring it to me, and I shall show you all I can."

Lancelot nodded once.

No one paid them any heed as they entered the castle. Guinevere expected to be taken to the dungeons, but instead Lancelot carried her to a small, spare chamber that held a narrow bed, a chest, and little else.

"Please, stay here, until I return. Rest, if you can," he said, moving to close the door.

"Thank you," she said.

He bowed. "I am only doing my duty, my queen." The door closed, leaving her alone with the evening light streaming in through the high window.

A window open to the sky, and a door he had not locked. Definitely not a dungeon.

Guinevere looked longingly at the bed, but she could not rest. Instead, she paced the narrow chamber, seven steps up and another seven back, until she caught her toe on the side of the chest and swore.

She kicked it, and the lid fell open.

A blazon of azure blue, embroidered with a silver sword, sat on top. Lancelot's, which made this his chamber. Why had he brought her here?

He soon returned, carrying a sack full of clothes and the mirror.

"I think it might be prudent to take you out

of the city, to somewhere safe, where Melwas cannot easily reach you. I would suggest Zurine do the same, but he cannot turn the city against her as readily as they turned on you, and someone from the royal family must stay to stand against him. King Artorius did not trust the man, and there were always rumours surrounding him, but...no one ever came to accuse him in court. That in itself is odd – why, I think he is the only courtier who has never had a charge brought against him. No man can be such a paragon that no one complains about him."

Guinevere smiled faintly. "How many times have you been accused of a crime in court?" Not once, she was willing to wager.

"At least once a month," Lancelot said. "More, if Sir Hector's gout is not bothering him."

She blinked in surprise. "With what imagined crime?"

It was Lancelot's turn to smile. "'Tis always the same. I offered Sir Kay or Sir Hector a mortal insult, and one or the other demands reparation."

"Which guards were they?" she asked.

"Oh, I would not trust either of them to guard your chamber, my queen, so you may not have met them. They are both arguably the worst swordsmen in His Majesty's troop of knights. Perhaps even the whole kingdom. Sir Hector was once tolerable, but he has grown soft at court, and between his girth and his gout, his balance is not what it was. Sir Kay...well, we were fostered together in Sir Hector's household. He is built like a bull, and he charges into every battle with all the finesse of a battering ram. In a swordfight against an opponent with the slightest bit of skill...he wouldn't last three seconds. Both men take any comment on their lack of sword skills as a mortal insult, up to and including the simple statement that I've won a training bout against either one of them." He shrugged. "One of them would bring a complaint, and the King would listen with more patience than I confess to owning, before ordering us to conduct a trial by combat, as is customary among knights for lesser crimes such as these."

"Trials you won easily," Guinevere guessed.

"A man must defend his honour," Lancelot replied matter-of-factly, before his expression tightened. "As must you, my queen. You accused Melwas of killing the King. While I believe there is much to distrust about the man, I did not think him so without scruples as to kill his kinsman."

She set the sack on the floor and took the mirror in both hands. "Show me the King's final moments, before he died," she instructed the looking glass. When the glass misted, she held it up so that Lancelot might see what it showed.

Guinevere wanted to turn away, but she could not bring herself to do so. Nevertheless, when she saw Artorius' grey, lifeless face, she was conscious of tears tracking down her cheeks.

A queen did not cry before her subjects, she scolded herself, swiping her sleeve across her face before Lancelot saw.

He sniffled and, to her amazement, appeared to wipe a tear from his own eye. "A terrible loss, both to you and the kingdom," he said. "His Majesty did not deserve to die at the hands of such a man. He would have wanted to die fighting, like he lived."

Tears flooded down her cheeks now, as she felt the barb of his reproach. "He did fight. I woke to him fighting his own body, that first morning. A body he could no longer control. To fight would have only killed him faster, and I could not bear to see him die. I saw the fear in his eyes…and I cast a sleeping spell over him. There was nothing else I could do. Yet…if I had not, and he had survived, perhaps he might have been able to fight off Lord Melwas. Maybe…"

"No, my queen. His physicians said he was dying. Perhaps you prolonged the end a little with your sleep spell, but the outcome would have been the same. To fall in battle is to know failure. Death in glorious battle might have been what he wanted, but he deserved better. You granted him the peaceful death he deserved, for few men have the luxury of dying in their sleep."

She managed a small smile, wiping her face again for what she swore would be the last time. "Thank you for your kind words of comfort, Sir Lancelot. I am…grateful that you chose not to offer me a mortal insult instead."

He bowed. "To insult such a beautiful queen would be a crime indeed. But if I may offer a suggestion…" His gaze dropped to the sack at her feet. "I must speak to the princess before we depart, and make my men aware of what Melwas had done, but while I am gone, I pray that you use the time to dress in clothing suitable for travel. Stout boots, if you have them, instead of court slippers."

Guinevere glanced down. She'd lost one slipper somehow, between leaving her chamber and arriving here, and wisps of straw clung to the remaining one. She must look more like a slovenly stable girl than a queen.

As if reading her thoughts, Lancelot added, "There's water in the jug and a comb on the table, as well, if you have need of them."

Give her a day stuffing mattresses with fresh straw instead of the political play of life at court, Guinevere thought. If the knight had noticed how bad she looked, she must look frightful indeed. Still, she had her pride. She drew herself up. "Do what you must. I will be ready when you return."

Thirty Eight

Lancelot found Zurine in her father's chamber. The King's body was gone, taken to be prepared for tomorrow's funeral in the cathedral. For a moment, Lancelot wished he could stay for the funeral, to pay his final respects to the man who'd been the closest thing he'd known to a father, but he knew he could not. As if Artorius himself had stood there to remind him, he was a knight loyal to the crown, and he would carry out his king's commands. Especially his final one.

He'd thought the princess was too deep in

thought to be aware of his entrance, but he was mistaken.

"I still can't believe he's dead, Lancelot. Can you?" she asked, her eyes fixed on the very pillow that had stolen his final breath.

"The dead are never truly gone, or so the priests say," Lancelot said. "But he had lived a long and happy life. If he could speak now, I'm sure he would say it was definitely his time."

"But I never got a chance to thank him. He was so busy with his silly wedding that he didn't get to tell me my prince had come. So…I couldn't thank him." She sighed deeply.

"What prince is that, Your Highness?" he asked. For unless the man was hiding under the bed, he was nowhere to be seen.

"Prince Xylander. He saved me from…the men holding me captive. A true hero. He will make a wonderful king," she said. A dreamy smile lit her face. "Father found him for me."

"And where is he now?" Lancelot pressed.

She waved a hand aimlessly. "I told him I wanted to be alone with my father's memory, so he went to guard my chamber from assassins."

While she sat here alone, with no guard at all. Then again, this was the first he'd heard of any assassins. Well, except for Melwas, of course, but assassin did not seem the right word for the King's murderer. To call him an assassin implied there had been some skill involved. Still…only he, the Queen and Melwas knew of his crime, or so Lancelot thought. Had there been others involved?

"Who told you there were assassins in the castle?" he asked.

"The Queen. Well, I overheard her. Telling an assassin to bring her my heart, of all things. I fled from the castle. I could not live under the same roof with a woman who wanted someone to cut my heart from my breast!" Zurine pressed a hand to her chest, breathing hard. For a long moment, Lancelot feared she'd swoon. Instead, she engaged in a lesser evil – she burst into noisy tears. "Is it wrong that I want her dead?"

No. What he knew of Guinevere…she could not have done such a thing.

"Perhaps you misheard. Or mistook her for someone else…" Lancelot began.

Zurine sniffled. "No. She was in her chamber, and I heard her as clearly as I hear you now. I don't want her here, or at my father's funeral. Where is she?"

Caution held his tongue. "Somewhere safe," he said. "I will take her outside the city, into the forest, and see that she does not return." Let Zurine make of that what she would. She'd surely forget about Guinevere before the week was out, too caught up in her own new duties as queen.

Zurine nodded stiffly. "Good. I don't want to see her again. I can't imagine what possessed my father to marry her in the first place."

Lancelot rarely betrayed the King's confidences, but he suspected Artorius would forgive him, this once. "He suspected his time was short, and he hoped she might be a fitting companion for you, when you are queen."

He was inclined to agree with Artorius. Guinevere was more of a queen than Zurine would ever be. Guinevere's steadying influence might have helped Zurine to come to terms with being a ruler with responsibilities, instead of the pampered princess she'd been all her life.

The horror on Zurine's face said she most certainly did not agree with either of them. "Then my father had gone mad!"

No. Artorius had been quite lucid, that last night. As sane a man as he could hope, with perhaps a little more foresight than most. "I'm sure he did what he thought best," Lancelot said.

Zurine considered this a moment. "Maybe. At least he got me my prince, in the end."

Lancelot sighed. Too selfish to see sense. "Princess, I should warn you about Lord Melwas. He – "

"I am here to mourn my father. After the funeral, I have a wedding and a coronation to prepare for. Lord Melwas can wait until after that."

"But, Princess, this cannot wait."

She screwed up her face, in the obstinate stare she'd used for as long as Lancelot could remember. She'd probably shown a similar expression before throwing tantrums for her wet nurse. "Then tell it to Prince Xylander. He will be your new king."

A stranger on Artorius' throne. Lancelot knew his king had hoped Zurine might come to her senses one day, and take up her duties as ruler, but the girl's father had been too optimistic. Perhaps in a decade, she might grow up and into the queen her predecessor had been. For Guinevere had known her duties, better than Zurine.

He suppressed a sigh, and headed off to find one of his men to take a message to the prince, telling him to watch out for Melwas, who was suspected of killing the King. Let this new prince sort things out here, for it was no longer Lancelot's responsibility. Lancelot had sworn to see Guinevere safe, and he would do his duty.

Thirty-Nine

Guinevere washed and dressed in haste, so she had plenty of time to regard her own wan reflection in the mirror before asking it to show her Lancelot instead.

"I will take her outside the city, into the forest, and see that she does not return." His grim words and matching expression made her wish she hadn't spied upon him, but it was too late.

He'd saved her from a public execution, only to take her into the forest to kill her in secret, instead.

Guinevere had to face the truth. Her father wanted to kill her, her brother was too caught up in his new bride to care about her, and the man who'd saved her life intended to kill her at the first opportunity, for his loyalty lay to a crown she would no longer wear.

Her first thought was to run, but she knew her running days were done. She had nowhere left to run to, and even if she did…Lancelot would find her. A man bound by honour would not rest until he'd done his duty.

It was time to surrender to the inevitable. Guinevere was no fairytale princess, to be saved by some hero for a life lived happily ever after, filled with love. That was the fate of Zurine, and her ilk. Guinevere herself had been painted too clearly as the evil, usurping queen, who had time to enjoy her throne and crown for but a moment. Until the new queen replaced her at the end, and this was the end.

Lancelot returned, talking of the need to hurry. He made no comment on her gown, the same white wool she'd worn when she entered court that first time. She hadn't bothered with a veil, though she could hide her hair beneath her cloak if Lancelot said she should. He did not.

A dutiful daughter, then a dutiful queen…soon to be a dead one.

Perhaps that was the duty of all queens, to die young. Like her mother, or Zurine's mother Viviana. She would see them both soon, surely, and be able to ask them.

With her wrists tied together and attached to Lancelot's saddle by a stout length of rope that hung between her horse and his, Guinevere was left in no doubt that she was the knight's prisoner. The people of the capital knew it, too, as they parted to let them through, though Lancelot's frequent shouts that he was taking her to a place where she could do no harm and that she was under his protection drove the message home like a nail in the coffin that should have been hers.

Now, she would forever sleep in a shallow grave in the forest, while the wriggling creatures that lived in the soil came to devour her corpse…

"Are you cold, my queen?"

His solicitous tone startled Guinevere out of

her morbid thoughts. They were on the road outside the city, with the walls looming up behind her like a monster preparing to strike.

The shivers that wracked her were not cold. They were fear, the biggest monster of all, that had dogged her steps for longer than she could remember.

Why did she fear the end so? It was inevitable, after all. Why fear what she could not fight or stop?

"Here, take my cloak."

The thick layer of wool that settled on her shoulders startled her. It was still warm from his body, and his hands were warmer still as they grazed her skin to fasten the cloak at her throat.

"Why?" she croaked, her throat too rough for her voice to come out right. "Why are you doing this?"

Instead of riding ahead, he kept pace with her. "Because it is my duty. I swore an oath, and I am no oathbreaker."

"What kind of oath? To take me into the forest and kill me?" That's what Zurine wanted, for she believed Guinevere had sent

Xylander to kill her. Her fool of a brother, getting things wrong, only to save the girl at the last moment. A fate he could have avoided if he'd only listened.

"No, you have nothing to fear from me, my queen. My oath…'twas one I swore to the King."

"Artorius, or Xylander?" For a moment, she entertained a spark of hope. If it was Xylander…

"King Artorius, may God rest his noble soul."

Hope died.

"So we ride all night, or until I fall off my horse and you drag me behind you to my death? Is this how this ends?" she asked bitterly.

"No, we ride until we reach my preferred camp. We will stay there for the night, and ride on in the morning."

And that was all the answer she was going to get, it seemed, as he nudged his horse ahead of her.

Guinevere lost track of time as they rode on in silence.

Finally, when she could no longer hear or see the city behind her through the trees, Lancelot led her off the road, onto a bridle path through the forest. The path soon opened up into a clearing, with a firepit in the middle of it.

Lancelot set down his lantern beside the unlit fire and started to unsaddle his horse. Then he sat down to light the fire.

Still on her horse, unable to get down with her wrists tied, Guinevere lost patience. "Are you going to leave me up here all night?"

"Of course not, Your Majesty. I did not realise you would need assistance to dismount." He hurried over.

If she'd been the vindictive sort, she might have kicked him. "Normally, I can dismount just fine, but I do not normally suffer the indignity of rope around my wrists."

"Ah, of course. I forgot. Allow me to assist."

She expected him to pull out a knife to cut her bonds, but he untied them instead, coiling the rope up on the ground beside his saddlebags.

"No sense wasting a good length of rope," he said cheerfully, offering her his hand.

She ignored it and slid from her horse. "Of course not. Not when I'm sure you intend to tie me up again so I don't run off while you sleep."

"Where are you planning on running to, my queen?" he asked, heading back to the fire with a log to toss on the flames. "To the capital, where the people wish to burn you as a traitor? Or back to your homeland, which you were so desperate to leave you came to throw yourself on my king's mercy?"

She had no answer, so she stayed silent.

"If you had wanted to run, you would have found a way to do so long ago. You might have departed the morn after your wedding night, before anyone discovered the King's illness. Or you might have tried to bribe or enchant your guard, while you were trapped in your chamber. Or you might have taken your eating knife and cut your bonds, or simply slipped out of them, for I tied them loosely enough, under cover of my cloak, and ridden away, to wherever you pleased."

Guinevere reached down in surprise to her eating knife, sheathed at her girdle. She had not thought of any of those things. What did that say about her? A braver woman would have fought to survive, but somewhere along the way, all the fight had gone out of her.

She should have burned, and been done with it.

Lancelot continued, "It seems to me that you are done running. What you really want is to stop, and feel safe."

Damn him, the knight was right. Yes, she longed to feel safe again, like she had as a little girl in her mother's arms. Before the birds had flown. To never have to worry about someone wanting to kill her. "But we seldom get what we want," Guinevere said. She sat on a log beside the fire and stared into the flames.

Should have burned.

"Ah, but it is your lucky day, my queen. It is my sworn duty to protect you, and keep you safe. King Artorius had but one regret in his life, that he had not been able to protect Queen Viviana. He made me swear an oath that you would not meet the same fate. Where we are going, Melwas and his mob cannot go. I have in mind a convent, where you may live a quiet life to the end of your days. To reach the convent, we must cross my land, and my people are loyal to me, not Melwas."

"So I trade one prison for another, and you are my jailer." And her crime? To be in the wrong place at the wrong time, to offend the wrong men while the right men saved other damsels. Never her. At least he would let her live. That was something.

Lancelot coughed. "Actually, I had hoped you might accept the hospitality of my house, before going to the convent. I would offer you the freedom of the grounds, though I would caution you against swimming in the lake. It is quite deep, and cold even in the heat of summer. We have a boat, and I'd be happy to take you fishing."

"Fishing." Of all the things that awaited her at the end of this journey, she had not thought it would include fish. This was all too much. "Sir Lancelot, I – "

"Don't like fishing?" he interrupted. "It is quite relaxing. Not like hunting at all, though you may do that too, if that is your wish. My house stands in the late king's favourite hunting grounds, and he has not come to thin the numbers much of late…"

She wasn't sure whether to laugh or cry. Or what to say any more.

Lancelot gestured toward some blankets he'd spread out by the fire. "Forgive me. You nearly died today, and here I am babbling about deer and fish. I'm sure you need rest. I should have brought the King's pavilion, along with a bed suitable for a queen, but in my haste, I neglected such necessities. You have my word that tomorrow night, you will sleep in the royal bedchamber of my castle, on a feather bed finer than Artorius keeps in the capital."

"Thank you, Sir Lancelot." She rose and stumbled toward the makeshift bed. She was so numb she did not feel the cold night air, nor the hardness of the ground, as she drifted off into sleep.

Forty

Xylander sat in the princess's bedchamber, fighting both sleep and boredom, as he waited for her to arrive. Some guard he'd make, if he couldn't stay awake. After a while, he decided to steal a little sleep while he waited. She would surely wake him on her return. He stretched out on her bed, and lost himself to dreams.

Much later, he woke to a small, warm hand, trailing up his thigh.

Zurine had spoken of seducing him on their ride here, but he had not expected her to do so before their wedding night. Curious to see what she would do, he lay still, trying to keep his breathing even as if he still slept.

She slid his tunic up to his waist, before he felt the mattress sink beneath her weight. Her knee slid between his, pushing his legs apart, before her hand crept higher.

He should put a stop to this, Xylander told himself. They'd marry in a matter of days, so there was hardly any time to wait.

Then again, with their wedding night only days away, no one would know if they'd decided to do a little lovemaking before the wedding.

A hand landed over Xylander's mouth. Bigger, heavier than Zurine's.

"You can scream all you like when I'm inside you, slut, but it'll be too late by then. You'll be mine, not some prince's property. And you will be my wife."

That was definitely a man's voice. Which meant it was a man in bed with him, caressing his leg.

Xylander reached for his dagger, slashing it across the hand on his thigh.

A high scream rose from the man.

Xylander threw himself out of bed and seized his sword. He whirled with the blade, just as the man fell forward. The blade met flesh. The man grunted softly, then collapsed.

Xylander hurried to rekindle the fire, thrusting a torch into the flames so that he might see who his attacker was.

The man lay facedown on the flagstones, blood spreading in a pool beneath him. Xylander used a foot to flip him over.

He recognised Lord Melwas, but the man's dead eyes did not recognise him. Xylander glanced at the man's hands, but neither had any blood on them. The cut along the man's throat was clearly what had killed him, but blood blossomed on the man's tunic, as if Xylander had struck him a gut wound, too.

No. He hadn't stabbed the man in the belly. Sure, it had been dark, but…

Xylander glanced at the bed. A dark pool of blood marked the sheets, and in the middle of it sat…what appeared to be a small sausage.

Realisation dawned, followed by horror. Xylander wrapped his hand in the sheet, seized the man's severed appendage, and threw it into the fire.

He headed for the table, and poured himself a large cup of wine. He downed it in two gulps, shaking his head at the sheer insanity of it all. Then he took a deep breath. "Guards!" he bellowed.

He didn't recognise the two men who came running into the room, but he wasn't sure even his brother Lubos would believe him if he told the tale of what had happened.

"That's Lord Regent Melwas!" one of the guards gasped.

"What happened to him?" the other asked.

"I believe he came here, intending to attack Princess Zurine. However, he found me instead, and I do not deal lightly with assassins," Xylander said. He threw another log on the fire to cover the man's flaming cock before they saw it.

One of the guards coughed. "Who are you, sir?" He didn't look like he wanted to issue the challenge, but with the grim determination of a man who knew his duty, he'd done it anyway.

Good man. Xylander would need to know his name for sure.

"I'm Prince Xylander, betrothed to Princess Zurine." Oh, he hated this bit, but for Zurine…he would do it. "Once we're married and crowned, I will be your new king."

The two guards looked at one another, before going down on one knee. "Your Majesty."

A pause, before the one who'd challenged him ventured, "What would you like us to do with the body, sire?"

Xylander gave it a look of deep disgust. "Take it away before the princess sees it. There has been enough blood and death. I'd heard this was a peaceful, prosperous kingdom. But from what I've seen lately…"

The brave man managed a smile. "King Artorius was a great king, sire, before he fell ill. A good king and queen can build us back up to where we were, right, sire?"

Xylander managed a regal smile, the likes of which his brother Lubos might have been proud. "Of course."

Forty-One

"Are you fond of hunting, Your Majesty?"

Guinevere looked up from her food to find Lancelot's eyes on her. What had he asked? Something about hunting.

She shook her head. "Hunting was my brother's passion, not mine. I had a whole castle to see to, with little time for trips into the forest around our home. Besides, the only weapon I know how to wield is a knife, and there is very little honour in slaying something small and feeble enough to fall beneath the blade of my eating knife." She brandished her knife, plunged it into a piece of turnip, and popped it into her mouth.

Lancelot laid his own eating knife on the table. "I have seen men slain in battle with a blade no bigger than this. Skilled assassins can kill with blades far smaller and sharper. Why, if you had been of a mind to, you could have used your eating knife to slay any one of your guards, while they lay in an enchanted sleep of your making, so that you might escape from your chamber in Castrum Castle."

She could not suppress a shudder. "If you suspected such things, you should have taken it from me."

"A man who falls asleep at his post deserves to die. Such is the way of war."

"I fear I have not the heart for war." Nor the stomach for it, either. Guinevere pushed her plate away, sickened at the thought of killing a man simply because he slept.

"You need not fear anything here, Your Majesty. We are so far from any of our borders that by the time an enemy came near, he would have to lay waste to half the country. By the time he arrived here, I would see you safe within the walls of Castrum."

Where the people of Castrum probably still wanted to burn her alive. Guinevere managed a watery smile as she rose. "Thank you, I fear I am unwell." She closed her eyes as she fought the terror of that night, stumbling blindly away.

A warm hand engulfed hers. "Please, Your Majesty. Forgive me. I meant to reassure you, truly. I am a knight, not a courtier, and I have little experience with fine ladies."

Guinevere opened her eyes. He looked so earnest.

"I am not a courtier, either," she said softly. "Luckily, I wasn't queen long enough for anyone to find out."

Lancelot swiped a hand across his face. "I fear I have only made things worse. To remind you of your recent loss…I meant to distract you, perhaps amuse you, by taking you hunting, but if you have no stomach for blood, I cannot imagine even falconry – "

She stiffened. "You have hunting falcons?"

"The finest in the kingdom, Your Majesty. King Artorius brought his best birds here, and they bred true."

She hadn't flown a falcon since the day her mother died. Her voice came out breathless with longing. "Show me."

Forty-Two

He'd been about to suggest that it was time she entered the convent, for Lancelot had all but given up on seeing any sign of the vivacity Guinevere had shown before Artorius' illness. For two weeks he'd watched her, as she sat at his table, fading as surely as she'd done while imprisoned in Castrum Castle. Almost as if a part of her had died with her husband.

Was it because she was a woman, that she mourned so deeply for a man she'd barely known? Lancelot had known Artorius all his life, and missed him as keenly as any dutiful son would his beloved father, but he had not let his sorrow stop him from doing what was necessary. More than anything, he felt driven to action, to do the things Artorius would have encouraged him to do, for death's shadow lay upon them all.

She pushed her food listlessly about her plate, as if it no longer interested her. Not that the stewed mutton had been anything to tempt the appetite of a queen. She needed something to enervate her blood – meat from a swifter creature than an aging sheep. Venison, perhaps, or fresh pork from a wild boar.

Perhaps the hunt would do her good.

Yet she shot down that suggestion as swiftly as a sleeping swan on a frozen lake.

The convent it must be, then. The holy women there might be able to help her, for heaven knew he could not.

"You have hunting falcons?"

Had he mentioned the birds? He'd been rambling, trying to find the words to suggest she go to the convent, but he forgot it all in the spark of light in her eye.

The first he'd seen in far too long.

He drew himself up with pride. "The finest in the kingdom, Your Majesty. King Artorius brought his best birds here, and they bred true." Though it had been a long time since the King had had the time to fly his birds, and now he never would.

The spark in her eyes kindled into flame. "Show me."

Lancelot offered her his arm, a gesture he'd repeated half a hundred times since he'd brought her to his home. But this time, the way her fingers tightened around his bicep was different. Like one of his falcons closing her talons on prey.

Yet no prey had ever been so willing to be captured as himself at that moment.

"Have the falconer bring the birds out by the lake," Lancelot ordered, not wanting to expose Guinevere to the mess in the mews. His castellan had died during the summer, and he'd been too busy in Castrum to come home to appoint a new one. He would need to remedy that soon, or risk not having enough stores to last the winter. Perhaps he should take Guinevere around the long way to the lake, to give the falconer time to find perches for the birds.

"Your apple trees have a bountiful crop this year. Your blackberry hedges are doing well, too. I imagine your alewife will be very busy over the coming weeks." Guinevere reached up and plucked an apple. She bit into it, closing her eyes. "Mm, ripe already and sweeter than I expected. I'm surprised your men have not harvested these yet. Or is the grain harvest late this year?"

A queen who knew about agriculture? He'd thought ladies knew less about farming than he did. "I would have to ask my men. My castellan would know..." Or he would, were he not buried in the churchyard. Did he even have an alewife? He ducked his head. "Forgive me, my queen. I should know more about my estate than I do, but my castellan has taken care of this estate since before the King gave it to me, and he died recently. Alas, he did not impart any of his vast knowledge to me before death claimed him."

Her lips lifted in a tiny smile. "My mother told me most men do not look further than their next meal, and then only notice if it is missing. Those who have the most, notice the least. Too busy waging war and playing at politics, tilting at tourneys or clashing swords. Women are the ones who make the world work."

Stunned, he stared at her. He'd never heard her speak so openly before. His mouth was dry as he tried to work out how to respond to such a strongly-worded statement without offending her. Finally, he settled for, "Without women, none of us would be here."

"I understand men also have a part to play in the begetting of children." She patted his arm. "Rest easy, Sir Lancelot, for the world needs men, too."

He couldn't help it. He burst out laughing, then stopped, anxious not to offend her.

Her eyes danced as a wry smile touched her lips. "Are knights forbidden to laugh?"

He sobered. "No, but offending the Queen is frowned upon."

Another pat. "I think I'd be more offended if you do not laugh at my jokes, Sir Lancelot. Or perhaps it has simply been so long since I told one that they are no longer funny. If they ever were."

He longed to reassure her, but anything he said would be a lie. He wasn't even sure why he'd laughed, for her words hadn't been that funny. Perhaps it had been her tone…

Deep in thought, he walked beside her in silence to the lake shore, where the falcons sat, hooded and hunched on their perches. One perch stood empty.

The beating of great wings heralded the falconer's return with King Artorius' favourite bird.

"She's magnificent," Guinevere breathed, approaching the golden eagle without a hint of fear. She accepted a glove from a servant and slipped it on with all the familiarity of a skilled falconer. Then she held out her arm for the King's bird.

Lancelot held his breath as the eagle stepped from the falconer's glove to hers. Artorius had rarely flown the bird himself, complaining that the eagle was heavier than his sword. Yet Guinevere did not lower her arm. Instead, she lifted it, launching the bird into flight.

"Magnificent," she repeated, watching the bird soar out over the lake.

"In his cups, King Artorius would often say that Sir Gawain was the most lethal of all his knights," Lancelot said. "More kills than the rest of us put together."

When Guinevere laughed, it was like the first spring sunshine, after a winter of dark nights. "The bird is a knight?"

Lancelot's heart swelled in his chest. This was the beautiful woman who'd stolen his very breath in the King's court. More magnificent than any eagle.

"King Artorius held a tourney here, to celebrate Zurine's sixteenth name day, a few years ago. Many knights came, in the hope of winning a favour or token from the princess, including one who called himself the Green Knight. He was greener than I, as it turned out, getting his helm bashed in by a stray lance early on. He continued to ride, but in the next round, instead of aiming for his opponent, he headed for the King." He found Guinevere's eyes on him instead of the eagle now, and hurried to continue, "The falconer was bringing out the birds for some hunting after the tourney, and Gawain managed to get loose. Instead of flying away, though, the bird headed for the Green Knight. She'd seen her own reflection in the knight's helm, and sought to do battle with the bird in her territory, I believe."

Guinevere gestured for him to continue.

"Gawain fastened her claws around the helm, and pulled it off the knight's head. Now able to see, the knight veered away from the King. Thus, the bird saved him from the Green Knight's lance. At the end of the tournament, before the champion was announced, the King knighted the bird for saving his life."

She laughed merrily. "I had heard many tales about King Artorius and his knights, but never that one of them was a female bird!"

Gawain returned, her talons clenched around a bundle of brown fur that turned out to be a fat rabbit, which she dropped at Guinevere's feet. Ignoring the falconer's outstretched arm, the bird returned to Guinevere's glove, and the falconer hurried forward to feed the bird.

"Good girl, Sir Gawain," Guinevere crooned, stroking the bird's breast with her ungloved fingers while the bird's beak was busy. Then, as if some signal passed between queen and eagle, she lifted her arm to let the bird soar once more. "I prefer duck to rabbit!" she called after the bird.

Lancelot wished Artorius were here, to see the two together. The King would have lost his heart to the girl, as he himself already had.

For a girl who claimed she didn't hunt, she flew a falcon far too well for Lancelot's liking. "Where did you learn to fly an eagle like that?"

Guinevere shrugged. "My mother was fond of her falcons. Ever since I was a little girl, I remember watching her fly them. She promised me that on my fourteenth name day, I might learn to fly them, too, but when that day came, she'd entered her confinement. Yet when I went to see my mother that morning, she refused to lie abed. Her feet had swollen so that her boots did not fit, and her belly was so round I feared it would pop, but she meant to keep her promise, so she'd ordered the birds brought into the garden. All day, we stayed there, while she taught me everything she knew about hawking. It was wonderful."

Yet she'd left her mother behind to come to Castrum. "You must miss her," Lancelot said.

Her eyes fixed on the wheeling eagle. "Every day. Perhaps if she hadn't gone hawking that day, or if she hadn't fallen...to this day, I still don't know why she fell. The ground was flat and even, yet she was suddenly on the ground, in a dead faint, one side of her face sagging just like Artorius', that morning after the wedding..." She wiped her eyes.

Realisation dawned. "Apoplexy. You knew."

"Yes." She sighed and stared at her feet. "Mother died, some hours later, and the baby with her. I knew it was only a matter of time before the same happened to the King. When Mother died, Father blamed the birds. He...went mad in the mews, taking an axe to perches and birds alike. I tried to stop him, but his madness must have clouded his vision. He struck me, and I hit my head when I fell. When I awoke, all the falcons had flown away. He would allow no birds in the castle after that, ordering them shot on sight. Mother had always loved them so...and to lose them, so soon after losing her... After Mother died, I became the castle chatelaine, and was too busy to have much time for anything. In Castrum...there was Lady Ragna to run the place, while I had...no place..." Tears trickled down her cheeks.

He wrapped his arms around her, holding her as she wept. "You have a place here, for as long as you wish." Forever, if he had his way. Even as her tears soaked through his tunic, he'd never been happier, his heart soaring up there with her eagle.

Guinevere lifted her head. "Thank you. Every day I spend here, I find myself more reluctant to go to the convent you said you would send me to. Nor would they allow me a falcon, let alone an eagle as magnificent as Sir Gawain."

"Then stay here instead. Until I choose a new castellan, I will name you castle chatelaine, and you may order the estate as you wish. Including Gawain." His mouth was suddenly dry. "For as long as you desire."

There was longing in her eyes as she looked at him. He did not make the mistake of imagining it was for him. More likely it was his estate, or the eagle.

"And what happens when someone comes from Castrum, to make sure the traitor queen is safely imprisoned in a convent, where she can no longer harm the kingdom, and they find me ruling your household instead, as free as a bird?"

"Then I will honour my king's final command, and protect you with my life."

Guinevere shook her head. "Artorius would not have wanted you to die for me. You are still young, and with this fine estate…you should find a wife, have children."

Lancelot managed a smile. "There is but one woman I want for my wife, and I fear she stands so high above me, I dare not ask for her hand." Now he could not meet her eyes, or she would know.

"You're in love with Princess Zurine?"

"What? Of course not!" He stared at her.

She relaxed. "Then I see no impediment. As the leader of the King's knights, you are second only to the King himself. Merely ask the woman. No woman in this kingdom with any sense would refuse you."

Lancelot wet his lips. "She is a widow, still in mourning." Surely she would guess.

She drew in a sharp breath. "You fell in love with another man's wife? I can't believe your high honour would allow such a thing. And yet...if you did not pursue her...yes, perhaps I can see that. You have hidden depths, Sir Lancelot. Few men would resist a lady like you have. But now...if her husband is dead, you have only to wait until she is done mourning, and there is nothing to stop you from marrying her. Unless...she knows nothing of your love..."

Lancelot bowed his head, not daring to speak, for he knew not what he might say.

"Right," Guinevere said brusquely. "Then you have her mourning period to make your intentions known. She will be your wife before the year is out and I...I will retire to the convent, for a new wife will not want another woman around, running her household."

Lancelot's heart sank. How had she

misunderstood so completely?

"My queen…" he began, not sure how to continue.

Guinevere waved her hand. "You have been kindness itself, Sir Lancelot. It would be cruel indeed to stand in the way of your happiness, and for all my sins, cruelty is not one of them. Merely say the word, and I shall yield to your wife, as readily as she must yield to you." She lifted her arm as the eagle returned, carrying a particularly plump duck.

Guinevere was too busy praising the bird and dealing with her gift to have any attention for Lancelot, or the proposal that lingered on his lips. Better that he never ask, for to have her in his household, to see her every day, would be enough…he daren't risk losing her. The lady he loved, who would never love him in return.

To be near her was enough.

Forty-Three

Guinevere was true to her word, giving orders to the household for all the world like it was her own. At first, she'd seen nervous glances directed toward Lancelot, before some of his bolder servants had summoned the courage to whisper their questions in his ear, their eyes fixed fearfully on the woman they'd surely heard was the traitor queen.

Lancelot nodded gravely at their concerns, but after the third such report, he held up his hands. "Queen Guinevere honours me with her care for my household. Without a castellan, we might not have stores for the winter. Out of the kindness of her heart, while she remains with us, she has offered to act as chatelaine to my humble estate. She has commanded royal castles, the staff of kings, including, 'tis said, the kings themselves. I am a fighting man. I know more of swords and arrows than turnips and preserves. Know that if she tells me to dig turnips, I will gladly pick up a shovel in her service. She is our queen, and we are all honour bound to obey her orders. Including me."

There was some laughter at this, but it quickly faded into silence. A round of nods passed across the hall, and Lancelot's people got to work.

Trees and bushes became stripped of their fruit, and Guinevere herself moving between the smokehouse, alehouse and kitchens, supervising staff who needed little guidance once they knew what was wanted.

She even had time to hunt in the afternoons, which became a regular occurrence when the cook ventured that she would make duck confit from Sir Gawain's catch. The eagle was as fond of duck as Guinevere, it seemed, and would happily bring her mistress three or four a day.

When the lids on the first casks of berry wine were nailed shut, Guinevere ventured into the cellars to take stock of what stores Lancelot already had. There was time to brew another batch or two of ale, and Lancelot's men wanted to send out a hunting party to bring back some deer before the first snows fell, as Lancelot was apparently particularly fond of smoked venison.

She sent the hunters out happily – by the time they returned, the smokehouse would be finished with the last of the hams.

Lancelot's wine cellar, however, was one place she hadn't been.

She descended the steps into the dusty cellar, wondering what Artorius would have thought of her venturing into such a dirty place. He certainly had never envisioned it, if the white gowns he'd given her were any indication. She hadn't worn any of her queenly attire since she'd arrived, preferring the gowns she'd brought from home. She'd need some warmer ones before winter came, and perhaps a new cloak, too. She'd speak to Lancelot's weavers in the afternoon, before hunting. She'd already met the seamstress who made Lancelot's beautiful surcoats. The girl's eyes had gleamed at the prospect of creating clothes for a queen, albeit a dowager one.

When she reached the bottom of the steps, Guinevere held her lantern high. Its light did not reach the far wall of the cavernous cellar. For a man who drank sparingly, there seemed to be an awfully large number of wine barrels here.

Back home, she'd have kept a tally on the wall by the stairs to keep track of the cellar contents. She surveyed the walls until she found what she wanted – faint charcoal markings that looked like they hadn't been touched in years. That would change.

She enlisted a pair of maids to dust the barrels so she could see their markings, tallying them up on a fresh patch of wall. The numbers matched for some of the vintages, but others had not been recorded at all.

A particularly large collection of dust-caked

barrels at the back, which all bore the same markings – a ring of what might be mountains or teeth, surrounding a smaller circle – had not been included in the tally. She estimated half the barrels in the cellar were stamped with this mark.

None of the maids, the alewife or the cook seemed to know what it meant, so she decided to ask Lancelot at dinner. Yet when she entered the great hall, Lancelot leaped to his feet, incensed.

"What happened?" he demanded.

She stared at him blankly, then glanced down to make sure she hadn't torn her gown on a bramble bush again, like she had earlier in the week. Combined with a particularly dark berry juice stain, she had to admit it had appeared rather gory to someone who hadn't known she'd been picking berries all day. Today, however, her gown was unharmed, but for a cobweb caught on her hem. She brushed it away with her foot.

"Nothing to be concerned about," she said finally.

Lancelot shook his head, then pointed at

her cheek. "But your face! Tell me who struck you. This will not go unpunished!"

She lifted a startled hand to her cheek, and it came away black. Guinevere felt her cheeks redden. "Forgive me. I was so caught up in my counting that I forgot to wash. I shall deal with it directly."

"Allow me." Lancelot beckoned to a servant, who brought forward a bowl of water and a cloth. He stroked the wet cloth across her face, his eyes so intent on his work that she did not dare lift her gaze to meet his, or she would blush even brighter.

Instead, she traced the spiky circle on the table with her dirty finger. "Do you know what this means?" she asked, taking the cloth from him so that she might clean the charcoal off her fingers.

Lancelot glanced at the table. "That's the mark of the kingdom of Moravia. Ringed by mountains, they make the finest berry wine in the world. So fine, only kings can afford to drink it. King Artorius shared a cup with me once, on the day he granted me my knighthood. It's a heady brew, sweet but potent. The barrels were locked in a special store room in the King's cellar. Only Lady Ragna had the key, and she guards it closely. They were part of the King's mother's dowry, I believe. She came from Moravia, along with Lady Ragna's mother."

Guinevere sat down. "Well, there are more than a hundred barrels bearing that mark in your cellar, covered in dust. Maybe more, depending on what's under all that dust. We couldn't reach all the barrels to read the markings beyond the first row."

Lancelot gaped. "In my cellar? A barrel of that is worth more than my whole estate. It's been a decade since anyone's been able to buy Moravian berry wine, and it was not cheap to start with. And there's…a hundred, you say?"

Guinevere nodded.

He paled. "You've just made me the richest man in the country. Nay, maybe the whole world. Marry me, my queen, for I'd be a fool to let you go."

He sounded so serious, but Guinevere knew it had to be a jest. She forced herself to laugh. "I only discovered riches you already possessed, Sir Lancelot. Hardly grounds enough for you to want an unwashed widow like me."

He opened his mouth as if to respond, yet he said nothing. Then a servant brought dinner, and the conversation quickly turned to duck, wine, and venison, and which would be wanted for supper today and on the morrow.

More than once, she felt Lancelot's eyes upon her, assessing her as surely as she'd taken stock of the contents of his cellars. Had it been anyone else, she might have turned away from such scrutiny, but she had few secrets left from Lancelot, and those were not worth knowing, anyway.

"Will you hunt this afternoon?" Lancelot asked.

Tempting though it was, she knew it was wiser to refuse. "I had hoped to, but I would prefer to finish my work in your cellars first. If I had known there would be so much already stored, perhaps I would not have ordered another wagon of mead from the convent. As it is…shifting so much so that I might see the markings may take me until nightfall. Or into next week. "

"I'll put more men at your disposal. I'd hoped to ask you to train the new falcons with me today, for the falconer tells me they are ready to start hunting. The birds can wait until the morrow, I am sure, but no later. I am...conscious that your kindness is far more than I deserve. I promised that I would take care of you, yet here you are, working so hard to ready my estate for winter. King Artorius would tell me I am derelict in my duty, and I fear our late king might be right."

Guinevere shrugged. "It amuses me to be useful. In Castrum, there was little for me to do, even when I was not imprisoned in my room. Here, I have the freedom of your house, the grounds, your cellars, and the use of your falcons. Here I am happy." As the words left her lips, she recognised them as truth. Unadorned, unexpected...yet so surprisingly accurate the thought silenced her for a moment.

Lancelot caught her hand and kissed it.

A tingle ran up her arm, just as it had on her wedding night.

"You honour me, my queen. I only wish your late husband had lived long enough to see you happy."

She sighed. Yes, she wished he'd lived longer, too. Always, Artorius came between them, a gulf that could not be bridged. "I'd best go finish counting your wine barrels. You might have another hundred barrels of Moravian wine…or enough vinegar to pickle ten years' worth of cabbage." She dropped a small curtsey. "I thank you for your hospitality, Sir Lancelot. I shall see you at supper."

Forty-Four

Xylander smothered what had to be his tenth yawn. It wasn't that listening to endless petitions from his subject was boring...but he'd scarcely slept more than half the night since he'd married Zurine.

She had insisted that a queen's primary duty was to produce heirs, and that meant he'd have to bed her two, or even three times a night. It was hardly a hardship – one look at her body stirred his desire, and her look of wide-eyed wonder every time she squealed with pleasure at his touch made him feel like the most skilful lover that ever lived. But a man needed sleep, too, or all the petitions ran together in his head, and he'd find himself nodding off in the middle of Hearing Day.

He'd wager Artorius had never fallen asleep on his throne.

Xylander pronounced judgement on the case – something about borders shifting, as a river moved its course between the spring floods and the summer drought – and the two men left, seemingly satisfied.

Instead of calling another petitioner, a knight approached the dais.

Xylander really did have to learn everyone's names. He knew every man he'd ever hunted with, so it shouldn't be too hard to remember the names of his new court.

"Sire, would you like me to call an end to the audience so that you may retire early today?" the knight asked.

The knight had seen him struggling to stay awake, then, though he was too well-bred to let even a whisper of his disapproval slip into his tone.

Yes, but Zurine would only see that as an

excuse to take him to bed even earlier. Xylander heartily wished that he could split himself in two – one to bed Zurine whenever she demanded it, one to do all the kingly duties that came with the crown that weighed heavily on his head, though he had not worn the thing today...and perhaps even a third copy, to sleep, go hunting, and do all the things he'd normally filled his time with, before becoming King of Castrum.

So... "No, Sir..." Xylander racked his brain for the man's name.

"Dagonet," the knight supplied.

"Thank you, Sir Dagonet, but no. These good people have waited many days, through Artorius' illness and our coronation, to have their grievances aired. The audience will continue until sunset, as I have promised." Xylander would show them that he might not be as good and wise a king as Artorius, but he would at least keep his word.

"Perhaps a restorative from the kitchens might help you, sire?" At Xylander's eager nod, Sir Dagonet gestured for a servant to see to it.

The next petitioner was called: "A

messenger from the King of Flamand."

Xylander's belly curled in dread. The last messenger had brought another man's severed head – a declaration of war from his father, for the head had once been attached to the shoulders of one of the King of Castrum's messengers.

The messenger bowed low. "Your Majesty, I bring greetings from the King of Flamand…"

Xylander squinted at the man. "Nunzio? When did you become a messenger?"

The last time he'd seen Nunzio, the man had been one of his father's guard captains. The bastard born son of one of Father's barons, he'd been considered noble enough to command men, but not quite noble enough to attend court. He'd greeted Xylander at the gates more than once, when his successful hunting parties had returned to the city.

Nunzio lifted his head, and stared. "Prince Xylander? What are you doing here?"

Sir Dagonet made a noise of disapproval. "You might be a foreigner here, Messenger of Flamand, but His Majesty, King Xylander, still deserves your courtesy as long as you are permitted in his court."

Nunzio blinked. He always had been a quick thinker. "Forgive me, King Xylander. I bring greetings from King Lubos of Flamand. He is anxious to reestablish ties of friendship between our two nations. He seeks his sister, Princess Guinevere, who he believes his father may have sent here. As King Ludgar lost his mind to madness in the end, he confided in no one in the days leading up to his death. King Lubos holds out hope that she might be found in Castrum, and he wishes to welcome her home to Flamand."

So Lubos didn't know about the marriage, or Artorius' death. Or that Guinevere had been crowned as Castrum's queen. Xylander wished he could be the one to tell the news to his brother, just to see his face. But they were both kings now, and he had no place in Flamand, just as Lubos had no place in Castrum.

"Guinevere." Xylander hadn't forgotten about her, but he'd been so busy, he hadn't had a chance to find out what had become of her. Some knight named Lancelot had taken her to a safe place outside the city, was all he'd heard.

The little he knew of Lancelot was enough for Xylander to be sure Guinevere was in good hands, for the man's honour was equal to his skills in swordsmanship.

But…Xylander should have sent someone to check on her, to make sure. He could send someone now, and set his conscience at ease.

That's what kings did – let other men do their bidding.

Yet…Xylander had not left the castle in weeks.

"How far away are Lancelot's lands?" Xylander asked Dagonet.

Sir Dagonet shrugged. "Two days' ride. Maybe less, if the rider is swift and does not stop to rest."

Xylander nodded. "Find Captain Nunzio somewhere to sleep in the castle. He shall have his answer in a week."

A week would be enough. Time to find out what had happened to Guinevere, and to decide what to tell Lubos about all the events in Castrum.

Forty-Five

One of the new pages came tumbling down the hill. He righted himself for a moment, before falling to his knees before Lancelot, his eyes wide with panic. "Sir, it's the King."

Lancelot struggled to remember the boy's name. All three new pages were orphans, and if he didn't remember their names, who would? Surely Artorius had never forgotten his name. He would need to make more of an effort if he aspired to be as good a foster father as the King had been to him.

"Slow down, boy, and tell me your name,"

Lancelot said.

The boy obediently took a few deep breaths. "I'm Galahad, sir. My mother was Lady Elaine, and – "

The bastard boy, Lancelot recalled. Lady Elaine had died in childbed, never revealing the name of the boy's father. Now he'd taken the boy into his household, there would be whispers that he was the father, but he'd never lain with Lady Elaine. Or any of the women at court. He'd hoped one day he might take a wife, but now...

Lancelot tore his eyes away from Guinevere, crooning to her new falcon. "Right. Galahad. Tell me what has happened to the King."

The boy's eyes widened even more. "He wants to know where Queen Guinevere is."

Lancelot's heart sank. He'd known this day would come, but he'd hoped to have longer before it did. The new king had consolidated his hold on the court quickly, if he had time to send someone after Guinevere already.

"See that the King's messenger is offered refreshment in the Great Hall, and I shall be with him shortly," Lancelot said. He hurried up to the house, praying that the messenger was someone he knew. A man who would trust his word, and head back to the capital while Lancelot worked out what to do.

"What is it?" Guinevere called.

"A messenger for me, nothing more," Lancelot called back. "I shall deal with him, and return directly." If he asked her to run and hide, would she do it? It might be the only way to save her. Artorius might have listened, been willing to weigh the woman's case before making a judgement, but this new king...Lancelot knew too little of him, and he'd heard very little from court. A man new to kingship might be swayed by his advisers, or Melwas...

Lancelot stepped into the hall, taking a moment for his eyes to adjust before he approached the messenger, who had a cup of wine in his hand already, and a jug at his elbow.

"Sir Lancelot," the man said. A man Lancelot did not know.

Some new servant of the King's, no doubt. Lancelot inclined his head politely. "You have me at a disadvantage, sir, for I fear we have not met. Yet my servants tell me you bring word from the King."

The man set his cup on the table. Now Lancelot could see his clothes were dusty from the journey – he had been in too much of a hurry to bathe or rest along the way. The King must want Guinevere most urgently.

"Not word so much as a quest. I have come in search of Queen Guinevere," the man said.

"She's not here," Lancelot said smoothly. "As I told the King, I took her to a convent where she might spend the rest of her days in seclusion. I shall send a servant to fetch her, though it might be some days before – "

"Xylander!" Guinevere's voice startled them both, as her quiet feet carried her into the hall. "What in heaven's name are you doing here?"

Lancelot's heart dropped into his boots as he sank to one knee. "Your Majesty," he murmured. What kind of king rode around the countryside alone, giving his vassals no warning of his approach? The man must be mad.

"King Lubos sent word that he wishes to

welcome you back home, and demands your safe return," King Xylander said.

"You can't send her back!" Lancelot blurted out, jumping to his feet, before he remembered to add, "Your Majesty."

The new king's gaze was as piercing as it was unsettling. "And why not?"

Because King Artorius had made Lancelot swear to protect her, and keep her from her family. His last command.

Lancelot swallowed. He saw no mercy in those cold eyes that he might appeal to. Then inspiration struck. "Because she is my wife," he said. "What God has joined, no man – even a king – may sunder."

"Your wife!" King Xylander exclaimed. "But the Dowager Queen is still in mourning for her husband. She cannot possibly have remarried."

How could Lancelot have forgotten? In desperation, he said, "Her marriage with the King was not valid, as it was never consummated. A mistake I did not make, I assure you, for she was still a maid when I took her."

He glanced over his shoulder to find

Guinevere staring at him, stricken. He only prayed that she stayed speechless long enough not to contradict the story.

"As her husband, I will ensure she has no further opportunities to commit treason, and that is why I have kept her here, away from the temptation of court. And here she will remain, as long as she lives," Lancelot continued. He didn't dare turn to meet her eyes. He prayed she would accept his apology, and his explanation, after the King had gone.

"And what has the lady to say to this?" the King demanded.

Now he heard her soft footsteps approaching, before Guinevere tucked her hand into the crook of Lancelot's arm. He half expected her to dig her nails in, as deeply as an eagle's talons, yet she did not.

"I like it here, and I intend to stay," she said. "With Sir Lancelot, of course."

Lancelot's jaw dropped. He closed his mouth as quickly as he could, knowing he would be too late, only to find the King's mouth hung open as he stared at Guinevere.

"Sir Lancelot and his falconer have been

training three new hawks, and I hope to hunt with them before long. He has promised me one for my own, and I believe I shall call her Circe."

The King grinned. "Hunting falcons? I should like to see the mews."

"Perhaps Sir Lancelot can arrange a hunting party for you and your new queen, when the new birds are trained," Guinevere continued. She beckoned to a servant. "Have chambers and a bath prepared for the King."

To Lancelot's relief, the maid hurried off to obey, without so much as a questioning look to himself. As if Guinevere truly was the mistress of this castle, as his lady wife.

"Alas, I cannot stay for more than a night. I must return to the capital in the morning. But perhaps, in the summer, a hunting party..." Xylander nodded, looking eager.

Lancelot nodded with him, trying to hide his dread. "As Your Majesty wishes, of course."

The King poured himself another cup of wine, and peppered Lancelot with questions about the hunting hereabouts, which Lancelot was all too happy to answer. This was King

Artorius' favourite hunting grounds, and Lancelot had taken great care to ensure his lands remained exactly as Artorius had liked them.

Finally, a servant came to escort the King to his chamber. Only when Xylander had vanished from sight did Lancelot bury his head in his hands. This was a disaster. He could not imagine anything worse.

A light hand touched his elbow.

"If you value your head, you'll come with me to the lake, where no one will hear us. Now."

Lancelot lifted his head to meet Guinevere's unforgiving gaze.

Things were indeed worse.

Forty-Six

As she led the way to the lake, Guinevere debated what to say first.

Yet it was Lancelot who broke the silence. "What possessed you to invite the King hunting?" he hissed.

Guinevere folded her arms across her breasts. "A more benevolent spirit than the one who inspired you to lie to him!" she returned hotly. "I'd thought you a man of honour, yet you seem happy to tell blatant lies to your king!"

"My king died in his bed before we left the

capital, and I never lied to him in my life," Lancelot declared. "That man might be his replacement, but he is not yet my king. I have sworn no oaths, pledged no allegiance…"

"Xylander is not a fool! It is only a matter of time until he realises that of all his vassals, you have not renewed your oath to the crown. He will summon you to court, and what will you do then?" Thoughts of Lancelot refusing to bow to the King, and having his head lopped from his shoulders sent her heart stuttering in her chest.

"If his summons is for me alone, and he is worthy to wear that crown, then I will swear any oath he asks," Lancelot said. "As long as he leaves you alone. Which is why I cannot believe you invited the man hunting. Here! Where you are hiding from the court. And drawing attention to yourself, appearing in the hall and addressing him directly – without his title! I asked you to wait outside, where he might not see you. Why, it is almost as if you wish to be tried for treason!"

Xylander would as soon cut off his own hand as try her for treason, as Guinevere well knew. He had risked his life to whisk her out of her father's kingdom to here. Was it possible that Lancelot did not know who Xylander was? Then again, perhaps Xylander was the one who had kept their relationship quiet, not wishing to alert his new people that his sister was the woman they'd tried to burn for treason.

"No more than you! Why did you tell him we were married?" she demanded. "I thought you lusted after some highborn widow, waiting only until her husband's bed was cold enough before sliding between her thighs! Do you plan to take her as your mistress, as you cannot have two wives? Or will you lie to her, too?"

Lancelot stiffened, as if she'd slapped him. "No man of honour would dare come between a man and his wife. A man's family is his concern. And I would be faithful to you as your devoted husband. There will never be anyone else for me, even if our marriage is a lie. I said what I did to protect you."

So Lancelot truly did not know. "But Xylander is my brother. Marriage to me would make you his brother-in-law. A man who will never be far from his thoughts, because Xylander will worry that I am unhappy."

As she would be, trapped in a loveless marriage. But…hadn't he just said…?

"Your…brother? Your brother is the new king?" Lancelot dropped to his knees. "My queen, I beg your forgiveness. I did not know. I will go to the King, and confess everything. Perhaps…perhaps he will do me the favour of granting me a quick death, if you would intercede on my behalf. I cannot ask for more."

He half rose, and Guinevere yanked him back down, landing in the mud beside him. "Don't be a fool! You can't go off without giving me answers. I deserve that much."

Lancelot turned anguished eyes to her. "Of course, my queen. What do you wish to know?"

The words didn't want to come out, but she forced them out. "My wedding night. How did you know?"

He reddened. "Perhaps you do not remember, but I stood guard outside your door that night. And…I listened…"

He'd listened to the King reject her and then start snoring. While she'd had her eyes closed, thinking of Lancelot. Guinevere's cheeks warmed, and she remembered Lancelot staring at her before Artorius had closed the door.

"What did he say to you that night?" she asked.

"He made me swear that if anything ever happened to him, I was to protect you, and not let anyone send you back to where you had come from. It was the last thing he said to me, and I could not disregard his dying wish." Lancelot met her eyes. "Even if it costs me my head."

No other man had ever been willing to sacrifice his life for her. A sacrifice she did not deserve. She could not let this man die to protect her. Xylander needed good men like Lancelot. If only she could spend the rest of her life with such a man, but his loyalty to his king came first, while a wife would always be a distant second.

"I absolve you of your oath. I will return to my father's kingdom willingly, and I'll tell my brother in the morning." Guinevere managed a smile. "My father is no longer king, if my other brother, Lubos, has taken the throne. He undoubtedly wishes to betroth me to someone, in order to rebuild the alliances my father destroyed in his madness. Some old man, who wants an obedient, young wife to give him heirs of royal blood. Or maybe just one who will keep his castle for him, and help to raise his existing children." Her heart constricted at the thought, but she knew it was pointless to resist. She was born a princess, a political pawn to be sacrificed for the good of the crown. If only Lancelot truly had married her. Only then could she stay.

Lancelot shook his head. "I swore to protect you with my last breath, and I shall. Even if it is from yourself, and your own brother. I will challenge him for you, for he will not take you from here while I draw breath. So I swore to my king, and I will not be forsworn."

Stupid, honourable fool! What man would rather die than break his oath? It would break her heart to leave him, but it would grieve her even more to lose him. Heaven help her, but she was in love with the man.

"Marry me." The words left her lips before she could consider them, and yet, she did not wish to call them back. "Marry me in truth, and live."

Desire flared in his eyes, hot enough to melt iron. Yet a moment later, it was gone, as if it had never been.

"My queen, I am not worthy. My king chose you as his bride, and I am merely a knight, risen in his service. How could I bring myself to sully the purity he made me promise to preserve?"

She'd been the widow he wanted. How had she not guessed until now? Now that it was too late. Unless...

Inspiration struck. "But I'm not your queen. I never truly was. The marriage wasn't consummated, remember? I am a maiden still." She swallowed. "When I lay in the bed beside Artorius, fearful of my wedding night, I closed my eyes and thought of you."

He stared at her. "Me? Why in heaven's name would you do that?"

Her cheeks burned. "I thought...if it had been you instead of him, I could endure it. If I imagined his hands were yours, that it was you touching me, inside me, I could bear it, nay, even enjoy, my wedding night." Why did she suddenly feel naked, with his eyes on her like that?

"Truly?" Hope kindled in his eyes, then died. "But your brothers – kings, both of them – would never allow you to marry a lowly knight."

"Actually, Xylander urged me to consider you, instead of Artorius, when we first arrived." She willed her cheeks to cool, but they would not. "Foolishly, I insisted a king would protect me better from my father's men than his most valued knight. I was wrong." She wet her lips. "Marry me, and I will tell my brother all you have done to protect me, out of loyalty to your king. I will keep your castle, be your chatelaine, while you continue to serve your king. Xylander needs good men, and you are the best."

Hope rose a third time, and this time it stayed. "And what would you ask in return for all this?"

"Me?"

"You offer me much, and even more to your brother. What is your price for all of this?"

Guinevere laughed shakily. "A princess is without price. I am a pawn, a prize, someone to be handed over to the winner in a game of politics. I don't get to ask, or to answer. My fate is to submit, to offer my body in service to whoever my brothers or my father deem worthy." Tears sprang to her eyes, and she wiped them away. "I am a woman, and my fate will be the same, whether I am a shepherd's wife or a queen. For my husband, I must lie back, spread my legs and bear his babies. Until it kills me." She wept freely now, remembering her mother, whose bed was barely cold before her father had popped a new wife into it.

Lancelot's arms encircled her, protective as always, as he pressed her face against his chest. Gentle hands stroked her hair as she only cried harder, wishing she could stop.

"You must think me ungrateful," she sobbed. "I have never wanted for anything, never gone hungry, never had to do more than choose which gown to wear. My father, my brothers, you, even Artorius, always took such good care of me. And I know I must pay the price for that. But sometimes I wish..." She sobbed harder, unable to finish. He would think her as mad as her father, to wish for what could never be. For women to choose their fate as much as men chose their own. To live free...

His voice rumbled beneath her cheek. "If you had one wish for yourself, what would it be?"

For herself? Guinevere almost laughed through her tears. Freedom was not for her. Finally, she lifted her head and said, "I would wish to stay. Here, with you. Where I might finish training those falcons, fly Sir Gawain every day, and one day share a cup of your very valuable berry wine with you when our first child is born."

Lancelot laughed. "You could marry a king, or a prince, who would give you wine and hawks aplenty. When any other man could give you a throne and a crown, why would you choose me?"

He already knew her secret, so Guinevere

did not know why her cheeks flamed again. "I never asked for a throne or a crown. I wished for loyalty and love, the happiness of a home. All these things you have already given to me. I choose you, because of all the men who might take me to their bed, yours is the only face I will see. You are the only man I desire. You, and only you."

He kissed her then, the heat of his lips melting hers as she gasped. His tongue stroked hers, as if to tempt her with what it would feel like if his body lay atop hers. She let out a tiny moan of longing. He took that as a signal to kiss her even harder, stealing the very breath from her lungs, until she had to tear her lips from his lest she swoon from lack of air.

He grinned, then cupped his hands to his mouth and shouted for a horse.

She stared up at him dizzily. "I do not understand." She'd admitted she desired him, something women were not supposed to do, and instead of answering her with words after that searing kiss, he'd demanded a horse?

"If we don't seek out a priest this very afternoon, I fear I will not have the fortitude to carry you inside, and even now I am tempted to make this lake shore our marriage bed."

Guinevere gave a nod. Yes. They had waited long enough.

She let him lift her onto his horse, before he climbed up behind her, then set off at a gallop for the church.

Forty-Seven

The feel of her soft body pressed against his almost unmanned him, but Lancelot merely tightened his arm around her waist and urged his horse on. The sooner they were married, the sooner he could start satisfying the desire he'd seen in her eyes when they'd kissed. He did not deserve a queen like her, but if he was what she wanted, then who was he to refuse her?

The priest had just sat down to an early dinner when they arrived, but a bag of coins and the promise of a whole goose to replace the stringy leg that sat on his trencher soon had him scrambling up to perform whatever service Lancelot required.

Lancelot repeated the vows after the priest, not remembering a word of them, so intent was he on the fever-bright eyes of Guinevere as she promised to be his wife.

It was a good thing the horse knew his way home, for Lancelot could think of nothing but the woman before him – his wife! – all the way back to the castle. He lifted Guinevere from the horse, and once he had her in his arms, he had no intention of ever letting go.

Forty-Eight

He'd bathed, he'd changed, he'd eaten…yet Xylander felt there was something else he needed to do. He wasn't satisfied with the knight's story. And Guinevere…something about the way she'd stood there, saying she wanted to stay, reminded him of the girl she'd been before their mother died, and Father went mad. But she was so much more than that girl now. She'd looked like the kingdom's rightful queen, not Zurine.

Yet when she'd spoken, it had been about birds.

Circe had been the name of Mother's gyrfalcon, he remembered now. The bird had terrified him, after it had nipped his finger, but Guinevere had wanted to take Circe hunting. Mother had promised she might, when she was old enough, but then Mother had fallen ill and all her promises had died with her.

Perhaps the birds, and the memories they held, had brought life to Guinevere again. But for how long? Xylander could not settle until he knew his sister was safe.

He drained his cup of wine and set it on the table. He would find her, and speak to her alone, without the interfering knight around. Her husband, if he was to be believed.

Guinevere would not lie to him. If she wanted a bird, or a whole flock of them, Xylander would give them to her, and cage them up to take them home with her. Lubos would not begrudge her some birds.

He beckoned to the servant. "Find Guinevere, and tell her I wish to speak with her."

The maid nodded and trotted off.

It was some time before the maid returned,

her cheeks flushed from hurrying to do his bidding. But Guinevere wasn't with her.

"Where is she?" Xylander demanded.

The maid bobbed a deep curtsey, keeping her head bowed so she wouldn't have to meet his eyes. "Queen Guinevere is resting, and not to be disturbed. When she is ready, I shall give her your message, Your Majesty."

The knight – Lancelot – was behind this, Xylander was sure of it. He'd given the order to keep Guinevere from speaking to him. Well, to blazes with that. A king outranked a knight – that much, Xylander knew for certain.

"Where is she?" he repeated. "Show me to her chamber!"

The girl squirmed uncomfortably. "This was her chamber, Your Majesty, until you arrived. There is only one royal bedchamber, so the master ordered her things to be taken to his chamber, as it's the next best, after this one. She is…in his bed."

Xylander cursed. "Show me the way."

The girl led him to a closed door, then took off before he could ask her anything else.

Xylander reached out to push the door

open, but it didn't budge.

He heard Guinevere cry out.

Resting, my royal arse, Xylander thought, putting his shoulder to the door. Then he put his ear to it, too, and he found he could hear another voice.

Lancelot.

"Yes, my queen," the knight said.

Silence for a little while.

Then, "Yes. Yes!"

Her cries grew louder and more shrill.

"Yes, oh, Lancelot, yes!"

Red-faced, Xylander backed away from the door. If Guinevere knew he'd spied on her making love with her husband…king or no, she'd box his ears.

Ears that could hear Guinevere's joy as clearly as if the door stood open, now, her cries were so piercing.

"Can I be of service to Your Majesty?"

Xylander spun. The maidservant who'd spoken was middle-aged and her knowing looks told him she'd seen all. Seen her king sneaking about like…well, like he hadn't done since he was a boy.

Xylander straightened, trying to look regal. "Inform Sir Lancelot and his wife that I had to return to the capital, and did not have time to bid them farewell. I will…send word when I can accept their invitation to hunt."

When he rode out of the gates, urging his horse to greater speed as if the devil himself pursued him, Xylander paused only once to look back.

Guinevere might not be happy when she found out he'd overheard her, but she was happy with her husband. Happy enough to make love with him in the middle of the afternoon, something even Zurine in her eagerness for children had not managed to do.

It warmed his heart to think that Guinevere would get to live happily ever after – maybe even happier than him.

As she should.

About the Author

Demelza Carlton has always loved the ocean, but on her first snorkelling trip she found she was afraid of fish.

She has since swum with sea lions, sharks and sea cucumbers and stood on spray drenched cliffs over a seething sea as a seven-metre cyclonic swell surged in, shattering a shipwreck below.

Demelza now lives in Perth, Western Australia, the shark attack capital of the world.

The *Ocean's Gift* series was her first foray into fiction, followed by her suspense thriller *Nightmares* trilogy. She swears the *Mel Goes to Hell* series ambushed her on a crowded train and wouldn't leave her alone.

Want to know more? You can follow Demelza on Facebook, Twitter, YouTube or her website, Demelza Carlton's Place at:

www.demelzacarlton.com

Books by Demelza Carlton

Siren of Secrets series

Ocean's Secret (#1)
Ocean's Gift (#2)
Ocean's Infiltrator (#3)

Siren of War series

Ocean's Justice (#1)
Ocean's Widow (#2)
Ocean's Bride (#3)
Ocean's Rise (#4)
Ocean's War (#5)
How To Catch Crabs

Nightmares Trilogy

Nightmares of Caitlin Lockyer (#1)
Necessary Evil of Nathan Miller (#2)
Afterlife of Alana Miller (#3)

Mel Goes to Hell series

Welcome to Hell (#1)
See You in Hell (#2)
Mel Goes to Hell (#3)
To Hell and Back (#4)
The Holiday From Hell (#5)
All Hell Breaks Loose (#6)

Romance Island Resort series

Maid for the Rock Star (#1)
The Rock Star's Email Order Bride (#2)
The Rock Star's Virginity (#3)
The Rock Star and the Billionaire (#4)
The Rock Star Wants A Wife (#5)
The Rock Star's Wedding (#6)
Maid for the South Pole (#7)
Jailbird Bride (#8)

Romance a Medieval Fairytale series

Enchant: Beauty and the Beast Retold
Dance: Cinderella Retold
Fly: Goose Girl Retold
Revel: Twelve Dancing Princesses Retold
Silence: Little Mermaid Retold
Awaken: Sleeping Beauty Retold
Embellish: Brave Little Tailor Retold
Appease: Princess and the Pea Retold
Blow: Three Little Pigs Retold
Return: Hansel and Gretel Retold
Wish: Aladdin Retold
Melt: Snow Queen Retold
Spin: Rumpelstiltskin Retold
Kiss: Frog Prince Retold
Hunt: Red Riding Hood Retold
Reflect: Snow White Retold
Roar: Goldilocks Retold
Cobble: Elves and the Shoemaker Retold

Lightning Source UK Ltd.
Milton Keynes UK
UKHW022210280219
338226UK00014B/861/P